givin' is a gift

BRIANN DANAE

playlist

This playlist is perfect if you like to listen to music while you read or after. Happy listening!

synopsis

As much as she tried to get into the holiday spirit, Mia couldn't shake her funk. A blurry night of regret had her questioning everything—her past, her choices, and the future she thought she wanted. Gratitude for where life had taken her was one thing; fully embracing its unexpected turns was another.

Then she met Bleek... again, and in real life. Charming and confident in his pursuit, Bleek treated Mia with a level of care and respect she hadn't experienced in a long time. Their connection felt almost serendipitous as if the universe had conspired to bring them together. Bleek believed it too—but convincing Mia was a different story.

Determined not to give up, Bleek was ready to show her she was worth the effort. But could he help her see the love she deserved, or was he risking his heart for someone who wasn't ready to receive it?

contents

note from the author

Hey! Before we hop into Bleek and Mia's story, let me just say this... you have not read this book before.

If you do feel that way, it's because the characters are originally from a short story I wrote in 2018 and then published in Vibez: Short Stories For The Soul in 2020.

No, you **do not** need to go back and read their story from that collection. I highly recommend, meeting them where they're at. This story is entirely different and continues their journey with changes, so don't skip any pages. You'll be seeing them in a different light.

The only books I suggest reading before this one are 'Spin 'Bout You and F**king Under The Mistletoe.

Enjoy, and Happy Thanksgiving!

Love, Bri

x

one

Trying to hold her composure together as best as she could, Mia stared at the screen of her phone until it automatically locked. It was set to blackout after two minutes, and that's how long she had been staring at it. *It* being the text thread from an unknown number.

The text thread was filled with picture "receipts" of what her man, Kaleb, had been up to. Despite who she thought he was, those text messages were proving otherwise.

Mia asked the girl to prove Kaleb was fooling around with her, and oh, did homegirl come prepared. She sent receipts of hotels in Kaleb's name, his debit card info that Mia thought she only had access to and pay stubs of an array of things Mia couldn't quite wrap her mind around yet. Kaleb's cheating, again, was too much. He had really taken things too far this time around.

"Mia. I know you aren't about to cry over this nigga," her friend Shay fussed.

Sniffling, Mia ran a hand over her cheek where a single tear had fallen and shook her head.

"No. I'm just... I'm just in disbelief. I mean, really?"

In a stump, Mia couldn't find the words to express her emotions. For so long, she'd scream, cry, fight, and be downright going to blows with Kaleb for the lack of respect he showed during their two-year relationship. Never having solid proof of his cheating until now, Mia was hurt. But deep down, she knew better. In fact, the lone tear that soaked her peanut butter cheek was out of anger. Pure rage shot through her frame as the screen lit up again.

> Just respect what we have and move on, sweetie. You need a man more your speed.

That was the girl's last message before she blocked Mia's number for good. Biting down on her bottom lip, Mia's nostrils flared, and her eyes turned into tight slits. Snatching the phone from her friend's hand, Shay scoffed in disbelief.

"Move on? What the fuck does she mean move on? She's the one playing the side chick," Shay grumbled.

"Is she?" Mia asked quietly, more to herself than anything. Looking at all the money and time Kaleb had spent with her, Mia questioned whether her role in his life had changed. *Am I the side chick?* She wondered.

"Yes, she is. Girl, that nigga Kaleb is wrong, but we knew that, Mia. You deserve so much more, boo. I swear my next relationship is going to be my last, or somebody gon' have to see me about their trifling ass son."

Mia went to reply and tell Shay it was cool, that she'd be good, but the opening of her and Kaleb's two-bedroom condo front door halted her words. Swaggering through the door like he had no care in the world and was the greatest boyfriend ever, Kaleb coolly brushed a hand over his waves and gave Mia a puzzled expression.

"Chu' looking like that for?" he pressed. He didn't even bother speaking, which said enough about his character.

Swallowing hard, Mia squeezed her eyelids

together. Her temperature rose, and the hair framing her neckline stuck to her damp skin. Peeling her lids open, she chuckled and looked him in the eyes.

"So, you still fucking around, Kaleb?"

"Man," he sucked his teeth. "Here you go. Got yo' homegirl all in your ear again. Is she fucking you too, Mia? I mean, let a nigga know since you always running with whatever she's saying. She yo nigga? She pay bills around this mothafucka?"

"I'm not, and nor do I pay bills, but another man can be," Shay said, mugging him. "When she leaves your ass-"

"No. It's cool, Shay," Mia cut her off and stood up. "I should have known he'd try flipping the script like I'm the bad person. Maybe I should be."

Kaleb's jaw flexed as the front door opened again. Mia wished he would've just stayed his ass gone. She was done this time, for real. Yes, she had said the same line for what seemed like forever, but she was finally done with his ass. One night of rest and some makeup sex she knew Kaleb would surely try to have wasn't going to work this time around.

"Damn," Shay mumbled when whoever it was stepped through the door.

Mia's eyes followed her gaze, and her eyes damn near popped out of her head. Thankfully, Kaleb had turned around to greet the man crossing the threshold of their home.

"You ain't got no manners? Closing the door in a niggas face," the man grumbled.

"My fault, man. You were taking all day. Anyway, this my crib. Bleek, this my girl Mi-"

"LaLa?" Bleek questioned.

If Mia could grant any wish of hers to come true, it'd be to disappear right at this moment. She needed Aladdin and his magical rug to come and swoop her the fuck up immediately. The lump in her throat went down roughly as she tried to find her words.

"You know this nigga?" Kaleb hissed.

"I, um. We've-"

"Yeah."

Bleek's dry confirmation made Kaleb look his way. They'd only known each other for a few months and were making good money together, so Kaleb was confused by how they knew one another.

Shay let the name roll through her mind, and her mouth dropped in recognition. A few months ago, she and Mia flew to the Bahamas for one of Mia's cousins' weddings. Let's just say Mia had a wild night. One that ended with Bleek's chocolate face, covered in the most delicious, manicured beards, buried between her legs before his dick dug her guts out. Mia had to cross her legs just thinking about the way he stroked her pussy to oblivion.

The way he groaned her other nickname, LaLa, out against the slope of her neck and trailed kisses down her spine made her body shudder. It was a shame how damn good a one-night stand could be. A one-night stand Mia had no intentions of ever reliving again.

Mia had put that night slash early morning behind her, and yet, here the man who gave her the best orgasms of her life was standing in her home. It was apparent he was an associate of her man. The man who had caused her so much pain. At that moment, Mia didn't feel so hurt anymore. She felt like Kaleb deserved to know she had fucked his boy.

"What you mean, yeah, Mia?"

Mia stood stuck with her poker face on display. She wasn't going to reveal that she had slept with Bleek. Not yet, at least.

"What he mean, yeah, Mia?" Kaleb asked again, his voice booming loudly.

"Stop fucking hollering at me! You're in no position to be questioning how I know someone when you've been cheating on me again!"

Bleek shook his head. He was over their little

spat already. He could have easily ratted Mia out, but honestly... that wasn't in his character. Plus, baby girl was sitting on a gold mine.

Her pussy was A1, and he had become well acquainted with her anatomy the night of her cousin's wedding. She had good conversation, too. Though drunk, he dug Mia's small talk before she took the initiative to engage in a sexual affair.

"I ain't come here for all that. I met Shorty out of town, tried pushing up on her, and she told me she had a man. You tripping for no reason," Bleek stated calmly.

His eyes were trained on Mia and the tiny shorts riding up her thighs. Seeing her fidgeting under his intense gaze made his mouth water, and he intentionally licked his lips while stroking the hair on his cheeks. Mia swallowed hard and broke eye contact when her clit decided to miraculously grow a heartbeat.

"Exactly. I'm so sick of your shit, I swear."

Kaleb waved her off dismissively. "A'ight, Mia. You so tired of my shit, but stay your ass right here. I ain't holding you hostage, ma. You can leave."

Mia stared him in the face and sucked her teeth. "You know what, I will."

"Okay, LaMia. Yo, Bleek. I'll be right back," Kaleb

replied before heading to their bedroom down the hall.

Shay sat silently on the couch, waiting for Kaleb to act out. She was with busting a niggas windows out, slashing his tires, and all of that destructive shit, but she'd help Mia jump his skinny ass, too, if that's what it came down to. What surprised her most was that Kaleb seemed to be playing it cool. Which she knew was only because Mia had evidence of his cheating this time around.

"You good?" Shay asked, and Mia rolled her eyes.

"Yeah. Can I stay at your place for the night?"

"You ain't really trying to leave that nigga," Bleek boldly told her straight up.

Mia whipped her head around and shot him an evil glare. "What?"

"You heard me. Your ass is all talk, LaLa. Oh, my bad. LaMia is it?"

Shay choked back her laugh as they stared one another down. Bleek wasn't in the business of taking what didn't belong to him, but technically, Mia had offered herself up to him. His mama, grandmother, and aunt had taught him his manners at a young age. He'd be rude if he didn't accept something given to him. The crazy thing was that he always seemed to fall for these types of women. The ones whose men had no clue how to care for them. That's where Bleek stepped in.

"You don't know me or what I plan on doing," she sassed, twirling her neck. "Who was talking to you anyway?"

Bleek's dick hardened. He loved that feisty, smart-mouth shit. "If you leaving, leave wit' me then since you so tough."

Mia's jaw dropped. "W-What? Leave with you?" A laugh escaped her lips after the shock of his words wore off. "Boy, please. I'm not going anywhere with you. I don't even know you."

"Nah," he chuckled. "You know me well enough. Just admit you ain't trying to leave."

Mia's top lip curled. "Are you making a bet on me or something? What's up with him?" She laughed, looking back at Shay, who was highly amused.

If he asked her to stand up and walk to his sexy, black ass, she was standing up and moving her feet as requested. It was evident he had somewhere better for them to be, and Shay wanted Mia to go with him.

"No, but we can now since you brought it up. Leave with me and I'll make sure you're straight on everything you need. Stay, and I get to sample that pussy whenever I want to. I mean, it's kind of hard to get that sweet shit off my mind."

Mia gasped. "It's been over two months since that night."

"Exactly. So, what does that tell you?"

"That's not even a good deal. What am I getting out of this?" she asked, flustered at his boldness.

"Me and everything else you deserve."

His answer was simple. So simple that Mia was conflicted. On one hand, she wanted to leave because dealing with Kaleb and his bullshit was a wrap. On the other hand, Bleek's offer, a lifetime supply of dick and anything her heart desired, sounded like a damn good deal. She didn't need him to get her on her feet, though. Mia was good on her own or with a man.

"I don't know, Bleek. This is crazy," she said just as Kaleb walked back into the room with a duffle bag on his shoulder.

"What's crazy?" Kaleb asked, eyes bouncing around the room. He felt left out and rightfully should've.

"You riding or what, LaLa?"

Mia swallowed hard. She had a decision to make and hoped it was the best one. If not, all hell was about to break loose. She could feel it in the air.

She stared at Bleek with pleading eyes, wanting him to shut the hell up. Yes, Kaleb was a fuckboy and deserved to get dogged out how he had been doing Mia for so long, but Mia's heart was too good to treat him like that. Well, at least it used to be. That one night in the Bahamas had changed her since. She was drunk, rambling on about how she wanted to be loved correctly and without having to be hurt first.

While they were laid up after some rounds of sex, Mia comfortably expressed her dreams to him. She told Bleek how she didn't usually move this recklessly, but the vibe between them was right. He was the perfect addition to her getaway. The one person who'd taken her mind completely off of the bullshit she called a relationship back home.

"I was just telling Bleek how crazy it was that we were related," Shay said, standing up from the couch. She was always going to cover for her girl.

Bleek smirked.

"Right. Did you know they were related?" Mia asked Kaleb, who looked Bleek's way.

"Nah. I ain't know nothing about that."

Though them being related was a lie, Kaleb didn't know a thing about Bleek except for the information he offered him. Bleek didn't even want to be working with the nigga to begin with, but his money was involved. Handing Bleek over the duffle bag, Kaleb stood waiting for him to look through it, but he never did. If the money didn't add up, his lifespan was getting subtracted.

"So, what's up? Y'all riding?" Bleek asked.

"Riding where?" Kaleb pressed, mugging Mia.

She rolled her eyes at him.

"To the store right quick, damn," Shay grumbled. She was beyond ready for her friend to end things with him.

Mia grabbed a pair of leggings from the basket of clean clothes by the couch and slid them over her little shorts. As she moved around the living room, Kaleb and Bleek watched her every move. It was almost comical seeing Kaleb look somewhat pressed about another man stepping to her, but there wasn't a damn thing funny. Mia was ready to show him who the leading clown of the circus really was. Sliding on her UGG clogs, Mia grabbed her purse and looked at Bleek. "So, what's up?"

Kaleb sucked his teeth and flopped down on the couch. "Bring me back a peach Vess, Mia."

"Mhm," Mia hummed, walking to the door.

Bleek didn't care what that man wanted, but he knew what he wanted, and *she* was leaving with him. He held the door open for her and Shay before letting it close. As she walked down the hall, Bleek couldn't help but admire her slim, thick frame. Mia's hips-to-ass ratio was ridiculous. Visions of her bent over the balcony of his private suite clouded his mind, and he smirked.

"LaLa," Bleek called out.

"What? With your crazy ass," she sassed, still walking.

"Say, LaMia. You better stop walking when I'm talking to you. Com'ere."

His polite yet commanding tone made flutters immediately appear in Mia's belly. Turning on the balls of her feet, her eyes landed on his muscled chest as he approached her. She licked her lips when he grabbed her by her chin and made her look up at him. The mug was still on her face, but she couldn't stop her erratic heartbeat. His gaze was so intense that Mia was sure he could hypnotize her if he wanted.

"Yes, Bleek?" she breathed out.

"What you got an attitude for? I did something to you?"

"You're making me choose between you and Kaleb, and that's not right."

"I ain't making you do shit you ain't already been thinking about. Did I make you fuck me?"

Mia gasped and slapped his arm. "Stop talking so loud! And no. You didn't, but still. It was wrong."

"Man, hush all that shit up," Bleek said, pressing his juicy lips against hers.

He was tired of hearing her ramble on about Kaleb's punk ass, knowing she should have been left him. Slipping his tongue into her mouth, one hand dropped down to her ass while the other held her still by the front of her neck. Bleek applied a little pressure like he had done while fucking her in his ocean-view suite, and Mia moaned softly. The grip she had on his shirt was sure to leave wrinkles. When she felt his bulge press against her belly, she backed away with erratic breaths escaping her lungs.

Bleek licked his lips, already missing the feel of her, and coolly stuck his hands in his pockets. His dick was so hard he couldn't think straight. "Let's go."

"Huh? Wait. Where are we going?" Mia was ready to get fucked. Badly.

"Um, we're still going to the store, right?" Shay asked with a chuckle following.

Bleek didn't even reply. He walked off, leaving

Mia and Shay to follow him outside. They whispered the entire time like young teenagers before stepping outside to wait for Bleek to pull his car around the front. When he rolled up in a Genesis Sport Mia had been eyeing, a mischievous grin covered her face, and her eyes sparkled.

"Oh my gosh," she gushed to Shay. "I love this damn car."

"Since he's calling out demands. Tell him to let you drive."

Mia smirked. "I sure will."

Bleek rolled his window down when Mia approached the driver's side. "Chu' doing?"

"Can I drive?"

"Drive what?" Bleek laughed.

"C'mon. It's so pretty. I'll go the speed limit."

Shaking his head, Bleek opened the door and hopped out. Holding the door open for her, he smacked her booty, and she giggled.

"You better drive carefully, too," he said before walking around to the passenger seat and relaxing.

The impromptu trip to the store wasn't needed. Shay threw that out there so her friend could have some privacy with Bleek. Mia pulled into the gas station parking lot and easily backed into a spot near the door. She smiled at how smooth the ride drove and peeped Bleek quizzically, staring at her as if he were trying to figure something out about her that she wouldn't confess.

"What?" Mia asked.

"You backed in so smooth," he chuckled, making her do the same.

Old habits never die. Mia's daddy and her brothers taught her how to drive and to always back into spaces when the parking lot or place was packed. It was easier to get out that way.

"And you were doubting my driving skills. I got us here in one piece."

"Barely," Shay jested. "Y'all want something out of here?"

Mia looked over her shoulder. "A sweet tea and a Snicker," she said.

"I'm good," Bleek replied.

Shay hopped out, and Mia shifted nervously in her seat. She wasn't expecting to ever be in Bleek's presence again, let alone have him pop up at her home.

"So," Mia began.

She wasn't sure what to say, but sitting in silence wouldn't cut it for her. Bleek felt the same way.

"How you been?" He questioned.

She wasn't expecting that question but answered anyway. "I've had better days, as you can see. You?"

Bleek nodded. "They'll return if you want them to. I'm better now." He licked his lips and smiled. "Much better since laying eyes on you."

Mia's cheeks lifted. "I bet."

"I wouldn't tell you any lies, La. You know that."

He spoke with conviction as if she'd known him well enough to trust him that much. Oddly, Mia felt like she did. Those few days with him in the Bahamas felt like a lifetime. She wanted to believe that she'd made his day better by gracing him with her presence but was having difficulty doing so. *Damn you, Kaleb*, she thought and sucked her teeth.

"We'll see. So, is this what you do in your spare time?"

Bleek's brows dipped. "Sit in the passenger seat of my car while a gorgeous woman pushes the whip?"

Mia couldn't help but smile. "You know what I mean."

"And you know why you're here. So, no. This isn't what I do in my spare time. It could be, though. With you... for you."

He picked up on the lack of attention and affection Mia was given. Bleek wasn't playing on her emotions; that wasn't the type of man he was. He was giving her the space, time, and opportunity to be open with him, expressing her feelings without obligation. Choosing to leave with him was a choice, but it wasn't about him in his eyes. Bleek saw the decision as Mia choosing herself; he just happened to be along for the journey.

Mia didn't miss the sincerity and the seriousness in his tone. He meant those words just as all the others he'd spoken.

"I like the sound of that," she said. "And I get you and everything I deserve?"

Bleek nodded. "Just say the word."

The problem was that Mia didn't know what she deserved. Not until this moment. It was eye-opening. She knew that going back to Kaleb was out of the equation. *He* didn't deserve her, that was for sure.

"Okay," she replied as Shay opened the back door.

Bleek's head tilted forward in a single nod. "That's all I needed to hear."

two

On their way back from the store, Bleek's hand crept up Mia's thigh while she drove. When he got to the top of her thigh and massaged it, Mia exhaled a harsh breath. Feeling his hands on her was something she didn't know she missed until now.

Her chest rose slowly, and her heart beat quickly. The heat of his palm was competing with the warmth of her sex, and she was sure he could feel it. When his fingers lightly brushed against the plumpness of her pussy, Mia cleared her throat to mask the moan she wanted to release. Thankfully, they were pulling up to the condos; otherwise, Bleek would've had her embarrassing herself. Mia pulled around back and parked.

"Call or text me tomorrow," Shay said, gathering her belongings.

Flustered, with his hand in between her legs, Mia said, "I will. Let me know when you make it home."

Shay told her she would and got out before heading to her car. There was no way she was about to blow her girl's cover by going back upstairs. As soon as Shay's door closed, Mia pivoted Bleek's way.

"You're bold," she stated.

"And you're wet. C'mere. Let me feel something."

Not having to be told twice or directed, Mia unbuckled her seat belt and climbed into Bleek's lap. His hands gripped her ass as she straddled him.

"Is it crazy that I miss you, and I don't even know you?" she groaned as his hands slipped into the band of her leggings.

"Not at all gorgeous. That's why this pussy is so wet?"

Mia nodded. "Yes. I've been thinking about you since that weekend. And this dick."

When she began to caress his dick through his pants, Bleek did the honors for her and unbuttoned his jeans, pushing them down his thighs. While she fumbled with removing his dick from hiding, Bleek acquainted himself with her soft lips. Their kisses were urgent, as were his movements.

He ripped the middle of Mia's thin leggings, scooted her shorts to the side, and slid into her gushy walls. Bleek cursed lowly under his breath.

"Fuck. Hol' up. Let me grab a condom."

Mia rotated her hips and broke their lip-lock to kiss his neck. "No. I want to feel you. Oh my gosh," she moaned softly. "You feel so good."

The head of his dick was so plump, and his girth was ridiculous. If Mia had to guess his measurements, she'd easily give him eight or nine inches. With how deep he was, length didn't matter. Bleek knew exactly how to hit her spot.

The way she was riding him had Bleek's head spinning. Wrapping one arm around her waist, he deep stroked her from below as Mia's body bounced atop his. Every time he thrust deeper, she bit down on his neck. Taking a handful of her hair into his hand, Bleek yanked her head back, lifted her shirt, and sucked on one of her nipples through her bra.

"H-How am I about to come already?" Mia whined, gripping his shoulders.

"Good ass pussy. You gon' come on this dick?"

Mia nodded.

"Nah. Tell me," he smacked her ass hard.

"Oooh! I'ma come! I'ma come!"

Bleek pumped into her, feeling his nut building up. He knew he should have worn a condom, but Mia had his head gone already. When her muscles tightened around him, Bleek let her cream his dick as her legs vibrated.

"Yeees," Mia moaned against his neck as she came.

Her breathy moans and snug grip around him only made Bleek's dick harder. Holding onto her waist, he bounced her up and down. Though it was dark out, her lust-filled gaze wasn't hard to catch. Mia fucked him back with enthusiasm and kissed his lips.

"I can feel you throbbing," she whispered against his mouth. "Let me feel something."

Bleek wanted to smirk at her choice of words she reversed on him, but the tightening of her walls made him lose all train of thought. His nostrils flared as he pounded into her and gave Mia exactly what she'd been needing and asked for. He hoped she could feel just how much he missed her, too. Breathing hard, Mia nestled her face into his neck and chuckled.

"That was... good as hell."

"Yeah... so, what's your answer going to be?"

Mia went to reply, but the vibrations from her phone inside her purse halted her. The two stared at one another before Mia reached over and grabbed it. Seeing that it was Kaleb calling, she went to ignore it, but the savage in her said to answer, so she did.

"Yes?"

"The fuck y'all buying? The entire store?" Kaleb's voice boomed.

Bleek smirked and patted Mia's leg so she could climb off him. Mia frowned and rolled her eyes before climbing into her seat.

"No. We're on our way back now."

"A'ight. Yo Mia. You know I love you, right?"

Mia swallowed hard as she watched Bleek grab some wipes from the glove compartment and clean himself up. Hearing Kaleb declare his love for her while having another man's secretions nestled between her thighs wasn't what Mia was trying to hear. Furthermore, loving her couldn't have been further from the truth.

"Mhm. I hear you. Know this, though…you need to know what you have before I be out of here. You think another man would treat me how you do?"

"Nah, bae. I know he won't. I hear you, a'ight? When you get back, we gon' talk." Kaleb said, looking out the balcony window where the parking lot was. He was staring directly at Bleek's car, but there was a heavy tint, and he didn't know it was his vehicle.

"Okay. We can do that."

Mia hung up, and Bleek hit the locks so she could get out. "Unless you trying to explain to your man why you don't have any pants on, I guess I know your answer, huh?"

Clad in nothing but her now wet shorts against his leather seats, Mia shook her head. "That's not fair, Bleek, and you know it. You ripped them on purpose."

He shrugged. "Heat of the moment. So, LaLa, what's it gon' be? You riding or what?"

"LaMia. You can call me LaMia," she replied in a huff.

Bleek smirked. "I take that as a yes then, Ms. LaMia, with your pretty ass."

He leaned over to peck her cheek, and her phone vibrated in her hand. Mia looked at the screen and frowned. She knew it was Kaleb calling back, but no name or number was present. The screen was a blur, as was everything in her surroundings, as Mia struggled to open her eyes. She fumbled with her comforter in search of her phone, frustrated with its constant ringing that had ruined a dream that felt entirely *too* real.

"Hello," she answered groggily.

"Mia. I know you are not still in the bed!"

Pulling the phone away from her ear, Mia wiped her eyes so she could see the screen clearly. Noticing her friend Grayce's picture and name, she hopped up from the bed but fell right back on it when her head began spinning.

"Ugh," she groaned and cleared her throat. "I overslept. I'm not late, am I?" Mia asked.

Grayce chuckled. "Almost. You have about twenty minutes to get dressed."

Mia sighed and slowly stood up. "Okay. That's enough time for me to shower and get dressed. The restaurant isn't too far from me, so I'll be there."

"I'm glad I called you," Grayce said.

"Me too. About blew the Apple off my phone," Mia teased, flipping her bathroom light switch on."

"Oh, whatever," Grayce giggled. "I had to. You sleep like a log."

"I enjoy my sleep, thank you. You interrupted a damn good dream, too, so you owe me a drink."

"Of course. Drinks on me. Well... on my man." Grayce chuckled.

Mia smiled. "He's in town?"

"Yes. He got here this morning."

Seeing her friend find love on a whim during a Friendsgiving cabin trip made Mia so happy. Grayce was such a loving and giving person. If anyone deserved to be pampered and loved on it was her. The fact that Jarod had flown into town to help her prepare for her Black Friday sale spoke volumes about the man he was and proved his devotion to wanting to see his girlfriend win.

"I know that's right," Mia praised and then yawned as she cut the shower on. "I'm about to hop in the shower, and then I'll be there."

"Want me to order you some food?" Grayce asked.

"Yes, please. Thank you."

Grayce let her know it was nothing, and they hung up. Mia stripped from her clothes and stepped into her walk-in shower. As the scolding water beat down on her, loosening the tension in her body, her mind couldn't help but drift to the dream she had. To her knowledge, her ex-boyfriend, Kaleb, wasn't a cheater, and neither was she. That wasn't in her character, nor was that why they'd broken up. Mia couldn't help but wonder if that would have been their fate if she stayed with him.

Then, her mind ventured to the man she had

cheated on him with. The details of all that went down were a bit blurry, but she vividly recalled how dominant and confident of a man he was and the way he'd made her climax. Mia smiled at the thought as she scrubbed her back. It'd been months since she experienced an orgasm like the one in her restful state of mind, but it was damn good.

Stepping out of the shower, she rushed to dry off, brush her teeth, wash her face, oil her body down, and get dressed. Thankfully, she didn't have to wrestle with her hair too much. The flexi-robs she remembered to put in last night preserved her almost two-week-old silk press. After doing a simple makeup look of foundation, concealer, eyeliner, and gloss, Mia exchanged purses and headed to her garage. She knew she was over her twenty-minute limit but was hoping some of the other girls were running behind as well.

Grayce wanted to treat her three employees and her friends who planned on helping her ship orders to brunch. With a much larger audience, more products, and a gang of inventory, she was going to need the extra hands. Filling their bellies while she went over numbers and their game plan to ensure things ran smoothly when the site went live on Monday was the least she planned on doing.

Mia was five minutes away from the restaurant when her phone rang, interrupting Coco Jones' flawless vocals and her struggling ones. She sucked her teeth and frowned. There was nothing worse than someone calling and interrupting her car concert. Especially since the person ringing her line should've been the last person hitting her up.

"Does this man not understand he's my ex for a reason?" Mia mumbled and begrudgingly answered, knowing he'd possibly call back.

When the call connected, she didn't even bother greeting him.

"Hello?" Kaleb questioned after a few seconds of silence.

"Mhm," Mia replied.

"Damn. What did I do to you?" He questioned as if he was her favorite person in the world.

Kaleb huffed, and she didn't know what for. She should've been the one doing the huffing, but she'd long ago stopped reacting to his emotions. That only seemed to add more fuel to the dimming fire.

"Bruh, I swear it's like you always have an attitude when I call you," he fussed.

Mia frowned so hard hearing him call her *bruh*. "I'm not your bruh, first of all. And that should tell you to stop calling me. What do you want?"

"I was just calling to see what you were doing."

Hearing her laugh pissed Kaleb off.

"I'm not sure if you've gotten the memo, but we are no longer in a relationship. Do I call you, asking what you have going on?" she asked.

"You could."

"I won't, and I don't care to know, Kaleb. I was being nice by not blocking you, but you're really making me reconsider."

It'd been months since their breakup, and since then, he's been trying to get back in her good graces. The thing was, there was no longer any room for him there. Had he tried as hard when they were together, they'd still be a couple.

"You gon' block me 'cause I want to check on you? That's crazy. Can't you see a nigga trying," he lamely pleaded.

"I don't need you to try. Honestly, I don't need you to even think of me," Mia told him.

Her answer was brutally honest and straight up, but that's how she handled him now. Nothing had changed. Kaleb was still manipulative, wanting it to seem as if he was giving one hundred percent of himself to receive credit for something he should've naturally done. Some days, Mia wished he would've cheated, but even then, she knew he'd still think he wasn't in the wrong.

"That's cold, Mia. How you expect me not to think of you when you still have my heart?" Kaleb questioned.

Mia chuckled as she pulled into the parking lot of Bistro. "I promise I don't have it. Probably never did. Isn't that what you told me?"

He hadn't said those exact words, but it was close enough. She wasn't the type to throw things in people's faces because they knew exactly what they'd said or done. For men like Kaleb, she had to bend the rules, though. A dose of reality was needed when dealing with him.

Flashback – 3 Months Ago

"You sure you don't need me to meet you over there?" Shay, Mia's best friend, asked.

Meeting her at his place would only cause more drama than she planned to, but it had to be done. Ending things with Kaleb should've been done months ago.

"I'm sure. I'ma grab a few of my things that I really need and give him his key back," Mia replied.

"Okay. I know I don't have to tell you this, but don't let him trick you into staying and getting some this is the last time, dick."

Mia rolled her eyes. Men didn't understand that when a woman was let down emotionally, they were turned off sexually. It didn't matter how good the sex was. Mia didn't even get aroused by the sight or smell of him. Nothing he said or did could get her to venture back down that path of destruction. Getting some dick was the furthest thing on her mind.

"Trust me, he can't even get a whiff of this pussy. I promise you."

"I believe you. Call me when you get back in the car," Shay said.

Letting her know she would, Mia disconnected the call and exhaled. The last time she had to break up with someone was in high school because they weren't compatible. The older she got, Mia realized that was a crucial factor in any relationship, not just the romantic ones. With Kaleb, her reasonings were different, yet they could also fit into the incompatibility category. At thirty-three, Mia no longer felt the need to constantly explain herself to a man—especially one whom she saw no growth in.

Using her key, Mia unlocked his door with a heavy heart but a clear mind. No matter how bad she felt about doing this, staying would only make her feel worse. Kaleb and one of his homeboys were watching sports on the couch. When the door closed, he glanced her way and smiled.

"What's up, baby? I didn't know you were sliding through," Kaleb acknowledged.

"Yeah. Can I talk to you in the bedroom really quick?"

She asked out of politeness, which she was all out of, but she didn't want to cause a scene in front of company. But she'd take it there if that's where Kaleb preferred to go. Mia was all out of fucks to give.

He glanced at the TV and back at her as if to say, "Don't you see I'm busy?". He didn't have to utter a word for Mia to know that's what he was hinting at. And that right there was exactly why she was leaving him.

Lack of attention.

Lack of communication.

Loud disrespect masked in quiet facial expressions.

Questionable remarks that shouldn't have hurt, but they did.

Mia shifted her weight, popping a hand on her hip. His friend looked at her and then at Kaleb before she walked off. If he didn't want to talk, she'd do no talking, just packing her belongings. Inside his bedroom, she stepped inside his closet and grabbed one of the duffle bags she owned. There were a few clothing pieces she couldn't leave behind, along with some perfume and shoes. Whatever else was left in her departure, he could do whatever with.

She felt him before laying eyes on him. Kaleb's presence was annoying more now than ever, and Mia didn't like that. Her body even responded weirdly when interacting with him. The tension... the unease. It was unsettling. Anyone who disturbed her energy without having to speak wasn't someone she wanted to be around, and Kaleb no longer deserved access to her protected space. She'd be doing herself a disservice by not honoring her body's request to eliminate the negativity.

"You going somewhere?" Kaleb asked.

Mia placed a pair of tennis shoes inside the duffle. "Yeah. I don't know how you'll take this, but we should end things between us."

He chuckled. Amused by her words. Mia didn't find any humor in them. She was dead serious. When she continued packing her things, the smirk fell from his face.

"Yo, you serious right now?" His voice raised an octave.

"Very serious."

He entered the closet. "Where is all this coming from? You woke up today and decided to break up with me."

Kaleb wasn't asking a question; he was stating the obvious. Truthfully, this wasn't the first morning Mia had these plans in mind. Today had been the lucky day. Facing him, Mia exhaled.

"I came home from my cousin's wedding four days ago. A trip that was planned for months. A trip you knew about and was supposed to be on with me. I somewhat got over the fact that you flaked on me at the last minute. But then—"

"I had shit to do, Mia. I can't just up and go out of the country because you want me to," he fussed, cutting her off.

Again, with the disrespect, she thought. Mia was too tired to explain that the trip had been planned for months, so she moved on.

"Okay, fine. I chucked it up and brought Shay. Whatever. The only, and I do mean the only thing I asked was if you could pick us up from the airport. You couldn't even remember to do that."

Sighing, Kaleb ran a hand over his head. "A'ight. That was my fuck up. I apologized. You gon' end shit with us because I forgot to pick y'all up? That's childish."

It was Mia's turn to chuckle. Now, she was the one amused.

"No. It's inconsiderate. It's selfish. It proves I deserve more from a man who claims he's mine but does the bare minimum in our relationship."

"The bare minimum? Man, you fucking tripping. I pay all your bills. Buy you whatever you want, and this what you pulling?"

"And you think that's grounds to treat me any kind of way?" Mia asked. "You're not here physically, emotionally, or mentally. What you do for me financially means nothing when you're not giving one hundred percent to us. Truthfully, I feel like the money you dish out is a cover-up for the lack of what you bring to the relationship."

His head drew back as he placed a hand against his chest. "Gotdamn. That's how you feel?"

Kaleb was hurt, but so was she. Mia nodded.

"It is. It's how I've been feeling for a while, and I'm tired. I don't want to fight with you or keep explaining myself. I just want to be done."

He licked his lips with a bob of his head. Then, his eyes squinted, and Mia knew exactly where this conversation was headed.

"This about another nigga? If you want to leave so

you can be free to fuck with someone else, that's all you had to say.

It was never about another man—just the man who couldn't get his shit together, which sadly happened to be him.

"Out of everything I've said, that's your conclusion?" Mia asked.

She was over this conversation and zipped the duffle bag to let him know it.

"Yeah, 'cause I'm not understanding why you coming at me like I'm the worst nigga in the world. Like I cheated on you or something."

Coming home late, missing date nights, ignoring her wants and needs, not taking accountability, forgetting important dates, and more was worse than cheating in her eyes. Stepping out wasn't a deal breaker for some women, but everything else was. Mia no longer wanted to delegate her time when she knew there was much better. Knowing she deserved more than what he was willing to give her. There was no point in having a man around if she didn't feel safe, feel loved, and had to do everything on her own. She might as well be single.

"I'm just letting you know how I feel," Mia said, brushing past him out of the closet.

"So... so. That's it. You just walk up in here and end

a two, damn near three-year relationship? I don't get a choice?"

It was comical how he now had all the questions. Questions Mia weren't entertaining. His effort was useless now.

"Not really. My mind is made up, and I wish you the best."

"Wish me the best? Man, fuck out of here, Mia." Kaleb scoffed.

He followed her as she grabbed her work notebooks from the dresser and unplugged her charger from the outlet.

"You ain't got nothing to say?" Kaleb questioned.

"Nope. Not anymore. I've said enough over the years. I'm done wasting my breath."

Her words were harsh, but she wasn't mincing them. Mia had done that one too many times. Pacifying a man's feelings was no longer her forte. It never should've been.

Kaleb sucked his teeth and said, "A'ight. Bet. You got it. This shit was all fake anyway. I could've stayed with my ex if I'd known you were going to pull this bullshit," he spat.

Uncaringly, Mia's shoulders lifted. "You could've, but okay. I'ma just grab my perfume and you can call her."

"Nah. Ain't that the shit I bought?"

She stopped at the threshold of the bathroom and chuckled. "Right. The same perfume you bought days after Valentine's Day."

He claimed he didn't know what to get her, but days later, he showed up at her job with roses, purses, multiple perfume bottles, and tickets to an NBA game. Mia didn't even like sports.

"That's the unappreciative shit my niggas be talking about," Kaleb grumbled. "I guess what I did was never enough?"

Mia ignored him as she hoisted the strap of her bag on her shoulder and walked toward the front of the condo. Answering his questions would lead them nowhere, and nothing she said would matter. They were over, and that was it.

"Damn, you leaving, my bro?" His friend questioned her.

"Man, shut up," Kaleb hissed.

Before she opened the door, she removed his key from her keyring and placed it on the counter. Then, she grabbed her key from the wooden bowl near the entryway and opened the door.

"Mia, come on now," Kaleb pleaded. "What do you need me to do? I'm not trying to lose you like this."

She'd checked out of their relationship long before now.

"You don't need to do anything but keep your distance like you've been doing."

With those parting words, she turned on her heels and walked down the hallway. Mia knew his pride wouldn't allow him to come after her, so she wasn't worried. A sigh escaped her as the elevator doors closed, and tears pooled in her eyes as the cart descended. They were tears of happiness. She put herself first for once, and she was proud of that.

"Man," he dragged. "I was upset. You know that. People say shit they don't mean when they're pissed off."

"Hmm. That's unfortunate for them," Mia replied uncaringly.

Unbuckling her seatbelt, she grabbed her purse from the passenger seat.

"A'ight. I get it. You don't want me calling you anymore. Can I at least text you?"

Now, he was really pissing her off.

"No. Now, bye."

Mia hung up and immediately went to block his

number before climbing out of her car. Inhaling a deep breath, she hoped like hell that Grayce didn't mind her drinking while they discussed business because she needed a few drinks now.

<h1 style="text-align:center">three</h1>

Unlike Mia, who indulged in a French 75 that was perfectly made, Grayce hadn't had a drop of liquor. But she thought maybe the bartender had accidentally slipped some Tequila into her lemonade. There was no way she'd just heard her friend say what she thought she'd said.

"Wait," Grayce giggled. "You did *all* of that in your dream?"

Playfully, Mia rolled her eyes. "Yes, and I'm confused because would I have done that in real life?"

Her words came out in a whisper, and Grayce chuckled. "I meeean… maybe?

"I don't think you would've cheated," Aspen, Grayce's cousin, answered before Mia could. "But getting your lick back with a fine man is my type of carrying on."

Grayce tooted her lips out. "It *was* your type of carrying on. You don't have to worry about that anymore."

Aspen couldn't help but blush. Her man, Ty Bentley, affectionately known in MLB as Turbo for the speed of his fastball, had shut all that down when he came home for Christmas a few years ago. Aspen agreed and was glad Grayce's employees were gone so they could talk freely.

"True." Aspen chuckled. "Had you not put that mistletoe in my kitchen, I'd probably still be single."

Grayce was the meddler out of the three, but it was for good reason. She wanted to see her cousin happy and not caught up over a lame, and she wanted the same for Mia.

"Well, it's too early to put one up in mine, so what's next?" Mia asked, making the laugh.

"Too early?" Aspen was appalled. "I put my Christmas decorations up the day after Halloween.

"Everyone isn't in the holiday spirit yet."

Mia's response was so dry, Aspen's mouth fell open while Grayce had a perplexed expression. "Mia... I'm sorry, I didn't mean—"

"I'm playing." Mia laughed.

Aspen exhaled and smacked her arm. "Girl. Don't do that. You were about to make me feel bad," she chuckled.

"Please don't. I'm just messing with you, but I am serious. That dream has me wondering if I should've cheated."

"Okay, Keyshia Cole," Grayce teased, and they broke out singing.

"I should've lied!" Aspen began.

Mia followed up with, "I should've cheated."

"Maybe I should've went out to the cluuuub."

They all sang loudly, bobbing their heads and waving their hands with their index fingers sticking out like women do when they're feeling a song. Thankfully, they were in a private room. That didn't mean much because a table of women on the opposite side of the glass doors heard them as they exclaimed remarks of *okay,* and *I know that's right,* urging them on. The trio laughed and continued their conversation.

"You can't take us nowhere," Aspen teased, sipping some of her water.

"Right. But Mia... the person the dream was about was kind of random, wasn't it?" Grayce asked. "I think that's weird."

Random? Yes. Weird? No. At least to Mia, it wasn't.

"You're only saying that because it's Jarod's cousin," Mia said.

"No, I'm saying that because when was the last time you saw him to be having dreams about him?"

Mia twisted her lips from side to side. She couldn't recall, but she was sure him popping up in her dream had something to do with scrolling his Instagram page the night before. Bleek's name popped in her notifications from liking one of her posts, and Mia ventured to his page out of curiosity.

Having met him a year ago at his and Jarod's aunt Moniece's birthday party, she wondered if he was still fine. And he was. Mia swiped through a few slides on two of his posts, admiring how delectable his dark skin was. Paired with a fresh fade and a smile showcasing pretty white teeth that lifted Mia's cheeks... she considered him trouble.

His masculine beauty, which she was sure was more than just looks, had her swiping out of the app and calling it a night before she double-tapped a post. The universe must've been trying to send her a sign. Admiring his pictures obviously wasn't enough. Homegirl needed to shoot her shot. She was single, after all.

"I only met him once, but he follows me on Instagram," Mia divulged.

"Knowing you, you were probably on his page," Aspen said, calling her out.

She knew her almost better than Grayce, and they'd been friends for seven years. Aspen had become family and vice versa. Had she not, Mia wouldn't have let her be all in her business.

"That's not a crime," Mia surmised with a smirk. "That man is fine as frog hair."

"You've seen a frog with hair?" Grayce asked excitedly, making them burst out laughing.

Aspen shook her head and squinted at the liquid in Grayce's glass. "You sure there's no liquor in there?"

"Oh, whatever," she said playfully, rolling her eyes. "Hopefully, y'all's buzz has worn off because we're swinging by the warehouse after this."

Extending her arms above her head, Aspen stretched and yawned. "Oooh. Would you look at the time?"

"Don't play. I'm not putting y'all to work that much today. I want y'all to see the setup," Grayce explained.

"That's fine. I don't have to be anywhere until later," Mia announced.

Grayce looked at Aspen.

"Girl, I was coming." Aspen laughed. "I need to see if the book sleeve I crocheted last night fits your new journals."

After finding her spark for sewing and crocheting again, Aspen turned her hobby into a side hustle. She wasn't looking to quit her job full-time like Grayce had, but she had enough daily orders to do so if she wanted to.

"You most definitely need to stop by. Mia, are you good to drive?" Grayce questioned, standing up.

Mia nodded. "Yes. That drink wore off a minute ago."

"Okay, good. I won't keep y'all for long, I promise."

Aspen and Mia looked at one another with a 'yeah right' expression. Knowing them, they'd get to the warehouse and start working. That was fine with Mia. Most days, she hated being at home alone. With it getting dark early in the evening, the holidays approaching, and being single, she'd rather be around her girls anyway. The more, the merrier.

four

The distinctive clinks and clangs of tools outside his office door were a sound Bleek would forever cherish. Knowing that the day was coming to an end made the noise that much more enjoyable. He leaned back in his plush chair, phone pressed to his ear, listening intently to one of his longtime customers on the other end of the line.

"I just can't thank you enough."

"Mrs. Darcy, you know you're welcome," Bleek said, a smile creeping across his face. "We do our best to treat everyone's ride like it's our own."

The elderly woman on the other end chuckled. A last-minute car repair at the end of last week stressed her out, but she was all taken care of now. Her gratitude spilled through the receiver.

"Well, you've done more than that, Mr. King. I haven't seen my truck run this smoothly since my late husband was alive and bringing it in. I'm driving down to Arkansas to see my sister for Thanksgiving without a single worry."

Bleek's chest warmed at her words. He remembered her late husband, Mr. Clark, and missed seeing his face. He was a cool old man who passed from a few health complications. Not once had Mrs. Darcy stepped foot in the mechanic shop when he was alive, yet she knew who Bleek was. So, he cared for her as if she were family because she was in his eyes.

"I'm glad to hear that. Enjoy the holiday with your family, and try to sneak me a piece of that lemon poundcake your sister makes."

Mrs. Darcy laughed heartily, reminding him why he loved his work. He connected with his customers beyond car repairs. "I sure will. Take care now, young man, and give your family my love."

"I'll be sure to. Drive safely."

Ending the call, Bleek placed the cordless phone on the receiver. It was the day before Thanksgiving, and the shop had been swamped all week. That wasn't anything unusual, especially with the weather changing. Owning an auto shop wasn't for the weak, and that word was nowhere in Bleek's character, at least when it came to his business.

King's Auto Care was a labor of passion and determination. Having grown up around cars with his dad, uncles, and cousins, it was only fitting that Bleek kept the legacy going. The family owned five auto shops throughout the city, and his was in the heart of it.

Running a hand over his waves, Bleek picked up his cell phone and saw a missed call from Jarod. He knew he had likely called to see what the move was for tomorrow. It was almost the same yearly, but the routine had changed since Jarod and Grayce became a couple. Still, they knew their aunt Moniece's house would be the last stop, family-wise, for the night. Before he could call him back, a knock sounded at his office door.

"Come in!" Bleek said.

Quincy, one of his youngest employees, entered the office. His navy-blue overalls were smudged in oil and grime, showing a hard day's work, while fuzzy shoulder-length locs were tucked under a worn shop cap to the back.

"What's up?" Bleek questioned.

"A woman is asking for you up front."

"She specifically asked for me?" Bleek asked

Sometimes, his employees passed upset customers his way, claiming they wanted to speak with him. Bleek didn't mind—it came with the territory—but he wanted to make sure.

"Yeah. Said her brother wants to talk to you," Quincy said.

Bleek shook his head. He hoped the woman coming in here with her brother on the phone an hour before they closed wasn't on bullshit. He understood it, though. Some mechanics liked to get over on women because they thought all of them knew nothing about vehicles. Bleek's prices were his prices regardless of the customer's gender. However, all business wasn't good, and he'd kindly turn her away if she decided to cause a scene.

"She didn't mention what it's about?" Bleek wasn't trying to go into the situation blindly, but it looked like that would be the case once Quincy shook his head.

"Nope. I don't even think she knows what's wrong with the car." Quincy chuckled.

He didn't find her situation comical, but the distress and confusion in her voice while she tried explaining was. Quincy knew whatever the issue was, they'd figure it out, so he wasn't worried at all.

Sighing, Bleek pushed himself up from the chair,

grabbed his cell off the desk, and pocketed it. "A'ight. Let's see what she got going on."

He patted Quincy on the shoulder as they made their way to the front of the shop. The scent of motor oil and rubber grew stronger, and the bell above the shop's door jingled as they entered the lobby. The smell was oddly comforting. Bleek could hear the frustration in the woman's voice before he saw her. *Another customer to help, another problem to fix*, he thought. Bleek's thoughts couldn't be more accurate.

"You're the one who told me to come here." Bleek heard her hiss into the phone.

She stood near the counter, shifting nervously as her eyes roamed the stack of car fresheners. Her face held the unmistakable look of someone who wasn't in the mood to be having car issues right now. Bleek's steps unintentionally slowed when he recognized who she was, and he couldn't help but smirk at her words.

"You have me up here asking for the manager like a damsel in distress. I mean, I am, but whatever. He's been back there for—oh."

Bleek came into view, cutting Mia's sentence short. She was just about to complain about how he probably didn't feel like dealing with her. That wasn't the case at all, especially now that he knew who needed his assistance. Despite how fine Mia was standing there looking with her dewy caramel-brown skin, round, pretty face, skin-tight jeans, and an olive-green fleece jacket on, Bleek vowed to remain professional. That was the last thing he wanted to do after scrolling her Instagram last week. He knew this had to be fate for her to pop up on him.

His easygoing smile didn't falter, noticing the surprise lingering in her brown slanted eyes. Bleek was just as stunned to see her as she was.

"LaMia," he said, nodding in greeting. "How can I help you today?"

Her brows furrowed, wondering how he remembered her full name, but not upset how it sounded falling from his mouth. Mia wanted him to repeat it so that she could commit his warm, velvety tone to memory for good this time. She blinked out of her trance, realizing he'd asked her a question.

Huffing, she said, "Something is wrong with my car, and my brother wants to speak with you about it. He swears it's my alternator," Mia said.

She placed the phone on speaker. "Dante?"

"I'm here," he answered.

"He's here. I'ma let you talk to him." Mia handed the phone over.

While Dante explained what Mia told him was going on with the car, she took the time to look Bleek over. The man in her dream had nothing on the one standing before her. His rich, cocoa-hued skin, plush dark brown lips, coarse mustache, and low-trimmed beard were so easy on the eyes.

Bleek was stockily built but not unflattering. His buff, muscled arms and broad shoulders stretched the fabric of his short-sleeved, customized Carhartt shirt, which had the *Kings Auto Care* logo embedded in the right pocket. One hand was tucked into the pocket of dark denim jeans that draped over black work boots. Mia noticed the dark ink adorning his arm. The mural only added to his attractiveness.

"Can you explain what the car was doing?" Bleek asked, making her snap her eyes up.

"It's acting like it doesn't want to drive. When I start it up, I'd have to really push on the gas with more force, but it was stalling."

Bleek nodded. "Is this the first time that's happened?"

"Kind of," Mia said and squinted. Bleek knew then that this wasn't a new issue but an ongoing one. "Sometimes it wouldn't like to start, but then eventually would."

"Would you have trouble getting the speed up?" He asked.

Mia nodded. "Yes! Do you know how annoying it is only to be able to go sixty or sixty-five on the highway?"

Her exclamation made Bleek chuckle. "Yeah, I can only imagine how pissed you've been. It sounds like the alternator, for sure. What kind of car is it?"

"An Acura," Mia sighed.

She experienced firsthand how much her foreign car's maintenance could run her pockets, but she wasn't getting a new whip. A paid-off car with routine labor issues here and there was far better than a car note.

"So, it's her alternator?" Dante asked, knowing the answer.

"Most likely, but I'ma have one of my guys take a look." He gestured to the counter where another worker stood and asked Mia to hand him her keys.

"A'ight. I know you don't be trying to get over on people, so I had her slide through there," Dante said.

Mia rolled her eyes. She appreciated him jumping into action when she called panicking but was still annoyed. Had he not moved out of town, she wouldn't be handling this. While he was doing all that delegating, Mia hoped Dante was footing the bill, too. At least some of it. That's what big brothers were for, right?

"Not at all. I'ma make sure she's good," Bleek assured, returning the phone.

He'd spoken with pure confidence, making Mia catch a chill and relax some. Her nerves were all over the place and she had somewhere to be within the next forty-five minutes, so she hoped he stood on his word.

"Bet. Sis, you good? Let me know what he says. I gotta get back to work," Dante said.

"Yes, I'm fine now. Thank you. I love you. I'll text you when I find something out."

He told her okay, and she hung up, sliding the phone inside her purse.

"Can I get you to fill out this form real quick while I have Ryan pull your car around back?"

"Yes. I didn't know you owned this place."

Bleek slid behind the counter, grabbed a new customer form attached to a clipboard, and handed it to her.

"Yeah. Family business. We got a few locations throughout the city," Bleek answered.

"That's so nice," she said, pulling a pen out of

her purse. "I'm sure customers like me make your job much more fun."

She was joking, and it was good to hear despite her circumstances. An extra bill sprung on you any time of the month was a headache, but a straight migraine during the holidays. Mia could've been in a worse mood, and Bleek wouldn't have blamed her.

Bleek chuckled. "Nah. It's the opposite, honestly. I love what I do. How you been, though?"

Mia scribbled her address in and then smiled shyly. "I've been really good, actually. I mean, besides today's woes. How are you? I haven't seen you since—"

"Since I tried getting your number a while back," Bleek interrupted, a slight grin playing on his lips.

Mia wasn't embarrassed about him calling her out, but her cheeks flushed. Glancing upward, she said, "Yeah... I had a boyfriend."

Bleek was happy to hear that he was spoken of in the past tense. Shooting his shot the first time they met ended with Mia politely declining his advances. He respected her answer because she had a man. Clearly, he wasn't man enough to know what he had.

"It's all good. I'm just playin' with you. We have

bigger problems to worry about than me hitting your line."

That earned him a soft laugh from her. "Exactly. But, I mean..."

He'd tried keeping it professional, but Mia made it difficult to stay the course. Between the intoxicating scent of her perfume, wild curls in her head, and those pretty brown eyes hinting at more than she knew what she was asking for, Bleek was struggling. He didn't see a ring on her finger, so he figured she was single-single.

"You mean what?" Bleek asked laughter in his tone.

"You were going to have to hit my line anyway to let me know what's going on with my car."

Mia hit him with the okey-doke, and Bleek chortled, shaking his head. "Smooth, LaMia. Real smooth, baby girl."

She blushed. "Mhm. I try."

Bleek wanted to tell her she didn't have to try hard but didn't. It was almost time to close the shop, so he focused on the task at hand.

"Make yourself comfortable, and I'ma go see if Ryan found anything."

"Okay. Thank you so much, Bleek," she said, tone much softer.

It was flirty and grateful—a dangerous combination that bulged the front of Bleek's jeans and stirred his heart. He kept his cool and told her she was welcome before heading toward the back. *Professional first. Always*, he thought. On his walk back, he couldn't help but wonder, since her relationship status had changed and their paths crossed this time, would there be a different outcome? It seemed like something more was there—a connection they hadn't had the chance to explore last time. Only time will tell.

And ten minutes later, it did just that.

Bleek stepped back into the lobby, wiping his hands on a towel as he approached her. Mia scrolled through her phone, texting Grayce and her best friend Shay. She looked up when she heard his boots against the tile. Bleek hated to wipe the look of hope and apprehension from her face, but he had to.

"Good news and bad news," he said.

Mia tilted her head, bracing herself. "Okay, hit me with it."

"Bad news, it's your alternator. The good news is we can get one ordered today."

Sighing, Mia said, "Okay. Well, can I still drive, or do you think it's unsafe?"

"I wouldn't suggest driving. The alternator

charges your battery, and since it's failing, the battery will drain quickly. You won't be able to start your car at all if the battery dies," Bleek explained.

Mia blew out a breath of frustration, and her shoulders slumped, trying to absorb everything. "I was hoping it was something small. I knew I should've brought it in when I first thought something was wrong."

"Don't beat yourself up about it. It's a common issue that can easily be fixed."

"How easily? I have somewhere to be in..." She looked at the time on her phone. "About fifteen minutes."

Bleek chuckled. "Not that easily. I know you don't want to be without a car for a few days, but it's for your safety." His words were gentle but felt like a sting. This wasn't the news Mia wanted nor needed right now. But... life. It had a way of slowing you down unexpectedly. She wasn't sure why now of all times, but there was nothing she could do.

"Ugh," Mia groaned and massaged her temples. "Thanksgiving is tomorrow, and I have so much to do today. Do you guys give out loaner cars or anything?"

The thought of catching an Uber or Lyft made her stomach hurt. Then, depending on others at such last minute was out of the question. She knew her friends would come through for her without question, but she didn't want to be a burden. Bleek kept a few loaners for situations like this, and would gladly put her in a reliable whip, but he had another option for now.

"What side of the town do you need to be on? I'll take you," he offered.

Mia blinked, caught off guard. "What?"

"I'm saying... it's already dark out, and I can tell you're not trying to have someone pick you up; I'll give you a ride."

Licking her suddenly dry lips, Mia wanted to scream no. Hell no, actually. *The last time I rode with this man somewhere, I ended up riding his dick. Absolutely not.*

Her brain was saying one thing, and her body was shouting another. They weren't on the same accord at all.

"Don't you have to lock up shop?" Her eyes roamed the place for emphasis.

"Nah. I can leave whenever I want to. Someone will lock up."

Mia exhaled. "So, a ride with you. You sure?"

"Yeah," Bleek chuckled. "You ain't gotta act like

I'ma kidnap you or something. I don't think that's my kind of thing."

"You don't think?" Mia asked with laughter, her eyes widening.

If only he knew he already had, she thought.

"Let me stop playin' with you. You coo' with that, though? If so, I'ma go lock up my office and wash my hands, and then we can head out."

Her hesitation was evident as she chewed on her bottom lip.

"You're not a bother," Bleek promised her.

He'd read her mind because that's exactly what she was thinking. Mia glanced out the window. She didn't have many options, so she agreed with a thankful sigh.

"Okay."

"Yeah?" Bleek asked, wanting to make sure she was okay with the arrangement. When she nodded, he said, "A'ight. Give me like five minutes."

He walked off but stopped and turned around when Mia called his name.

"Bleek."

"Yeah?"

"The event is on the southside. You know where the youth center, Impact, is?" Mia asked.

Bleek nodded. "Yeah. I know exactly where it's at."

"Okay," she mumbled. "I'll be here waiting."

A grin tugged at the corners of his mouth. She had other choices other than waiting on him, but he was glad she'd chosen to take him up on his offer. Once he locked his office door, all professionalism would be forgotten.

Mia was so happy she didn't have to call the event host and flake on them. She volunteered every Thanksgiving and some Christmas mornings when she could make it. Impact, owned by Krypt Priest, held many community events year-round, but Thanksgiving and Christmas had been the biggest so far.

When Bleek pulled his Yukon Denali into the community center's packed parking lot, it took him a minute to find parking. The community's families and friends had shown up to receive and give back, and Mia loved to see it. Her spirits were usually down around this time of the year, so she surrounded herself with love. Sometimes, community, even with strangers, was the best comfort.

Bleek cut the engine, and Mia's brows shot up. "You're getting out?"

"I've got some free time on my hands to help out."

Mia's eyes unintentionally fell to his large hands resting against his muscular thighs. She had other plans he could use them for. Neatly trimmed and clean nails on a man was one of her weaknesses. Thick veins aligned them, and they displayed his hard work of working on cars. Yet, she knew they'd be capable of offering her the softest, most reassuring touch after a panty-wetting smack to her ass.

Clearing her throat, she said, "Oh. Okay. That's nice of you."

Bleek shook his head. "Aye. You gon' stop trying to make me out to be weirdo."

Mia broke out laughing. "How am I doing that?"

"First, you didn't want me to give you a ride. Now, you acting like I don't have a heart for the community."

Laughing, Mia tossed a hand over her face to hide her wide grin. "I am *so* sorry for real. It's not like that. I'm just used to—"

She was about to go on a tangent about her ex, but quickly stopped herself. There'd been plenty of times she called Kaleb in need of something and he hadn't answered nor had an answer. He also never once volunteered to go with her to these events. So, it was refreshing and heartwarming to see Bleek initiate the deed.

"It's all good, beautiful. Remove whatever ideas you had about me from your head," Bleek said.

Mia smiled. "Okay. I can do that. No hard feelings?"

"None at all," he said and grinned. "Let's get in here and serve our community."

When she reached for the door, her body flinched at his abrupt outburst.

"What you doing? You didn't touch that door getting in, so don't touch it climbing out."

Mia quickly tucked her lips. *Okay. Check my ass, then,* she thought. Bleek walked around to her side and opened the door before helping her down. She was a tall girlie at five-foot-nine, but his SUV sat up so high it took some effort to get in and out of. Bleek was six-three, so he made maneuvering look easy.

Seeing her face light up as they approached the building made Bleek happy he offered her a ride. He could tell this was her element. As soon as they entered the center, they were warmly greeted by staff and volunteers. At the check-in table, they signed in and received maroon-colored t-shirts indicating they were volunteers.

"I'ma find the restroom and change into my shirt real quick. Is there a specific spot I need to be?" Bleek asked.

"Not necessarily, but you can probably be by the loading docks. Some families drive up instead of coming in to get meals," Mia explained.

While some community give-back events gave out turkeys to cook, canned goods, and food, Krypt wanted his to be different and more impactful. Some families didn't have a place to cook, while others didn't have time or weren't fortunate enough to go grocery shopping. So, he had people prepare meals to go, *and* you had an option to get free food items and beverages. Since he knew most places were closed for the holiday, the community outreach director printed off a list of locations that would be warm and where they could warm their food up.

Removing her fleece, Mia slid her shirt on and got to work. After squirting some hand sanitizer in her hands, she walked to the table where she saw a familiar face.

"Is this spot taken?" She asked, smiling.

Moraye turned to the left, and her cheeks lifted from smiling so hard. "Mia, hi," she sang as they hugged. "When I didn't see you here early, I got kind of worried."

"I had some car trouble, but I still made it. It is packed this year. That makes me so happy."

Her emotions were warranted. The number of volunteer shirts she spotted roaming around seemed to have tripled since last year.

"Me too! Is everything okay with your car?" Moraye asked.

Mia shook her head. "No, but it will be. It's at the shop. How are you, though?"

"Well, that's good. I'm glad you could get it in and checked out," she said genuinely. "I'm beyond good, girl. When I leave here, I'm headed home for a quick shower and a nap before heading to FRO."

The twenty-four-hour Black-owned bookstore, affectionately known as For Readers Only, was where they met. Moraye worked there, and Mia visited once a week—twice some weeks when they had new releases drop or an author as a special guest. Mia looked like a familiar face she'd seen around the center during events, and they immediately clicked once introducing themselves.

"Oooh. I know y'all are having some good sales this week," Mia said, already planning to make a trip. She had a few spots on her shelf that she could fill.

"Yes. Everything in the store is twenty-five percent off except special editions. Want me to put you some to the side to come get?" Moraye asked, already knowing she would.

"Yes, please," Mia urged. "Oh, wait. I don't have a car."

Her mood changed that quickly.

"I can still put them to the side. How did you get here today?"

"I um," she said and searched the area for Bleek.

She spotted him where she told him to go, carrying a heavy box of food out the side door where a pick-up truck was waiting.

"He just walked outside, but his name is Bleek. He owns the shop I took my car to," Mia explained.

"Awww. That was nice of him to bring you. Is that him?" Moraye asked as Bleek's head swiveled in search of her.

Mia swallowed hard when his eyes landed on her, and he chucked his head upward with a smile. She grinned back and waved.

"Yes, that's him," she answered.

"Whew." Moraye laughed. "I know that's right."

"Oh girl, please. Like Adrien isn't handsome himself."

Moraye giggled. "My man is fine as hell, thank you very much."

They fell into one another laughing. Moraye hadn't told not one lie. Adrien, her boyfriend and head coach of the basketball team at the community center was around there somewhere, working like the other men. Seeing a group of men, especially Black men, give back and pour into the community was what Mia considered a small part of healing the world. Even healing childhood wounds. It'd take a lot more than their efforts, but what they did do was impactful.

Two hours went by with them handing out to-go aluminum trays, canned goods, and some desserts. Mia's stomach growled with each savory whiff she inhaled. Wanting to find her plus one who hadn't checked on her in an hour, Mia's eyes roamed the floor.

Bleek was chatting with a family across the room, seamlessly fitting in. Mia caught herself smiling when he knelt to hand a young boy a turkey, making sure he could hold it, before hugging the mother a father. The mother mouthed a grateful "thank you" as they walked off, and Mia's eyes watered. She had to fan her face to keep from crying.

"You okay?" Moraye asked, removing a box pies were in from the table.

Mia nodded. She was too choked up to speak. There was something about the way he was moving around the room with utter confidence and politeness that had her wishing she had given him her number a year ago. Bleek wasn't doing this to look good— he genuinely cared, and it showed in the way the families *and* Mia responded to him.

Her heart fluttered as she stared him down. Bleek was oblivious to her gawking, but Moraye wasn't.

"You're staring and about to drool," she teased, nudging Mia's side.

Not thinking of it, Mia blinked and wiped the corner of her mouth while giggling. "Oh, my gosh. I'm down bad, and this is our first time hanging out."

"I'd tell you to stand up, but nope. Lay down... or bend over," Moraye giggled. "Whichever you prefer."

The older woman next to them grinned, overhearing their conversation. "If I had a dollar for every time I've seen that dreamy look in your eyes and smile on your face today, I'd buy me some scratch-off tickets."

Mia laughed. "Ms. Cynthia, you were going to do that anyway."

"I'm glad you know, sweetie, and I'm happy to see you in better spirits this year. Don't let the moment pass."

Her words made Mia's stomach flip in a good way. Grieving during the holidays was rough, but kind words like Ms. Cynthia's and bubbly personalities like Moraye's kept Mia going. Now, she could add Bleek's generous heart to why her spirits were up. She tried to busy herself and act as if she hadn't been staring when Bleek approached her.

"Y'all good over here? Need anything restocked?" he asked the table of six.

The women surveyed their inventory and told him no. Bleek focused on Mia.

"How about you? You good, beautiful?" He casually leaned against the corner of the table and Mia's breathing picked up.

"Yes," she said, clearing her throat. "You're... really good at this."

"Good at what?"

"Talking to people. Making them feel... seen." She gestured toward the families. "They love you."

Bleek shrugged modestly, though her words warmed his soul. "It's easy when you mean it. Everybody deserves to feel loved and seen no matter what walk of life they're on or going through."

Mia bit her lip, warmth spreading through her chest. She wasn't just impressed—she was captivated. Gotdamn in love if she wanted to be delusional for the day. It was perfect timing.

Bleek noticed her pause and tilted his head. "What?"

"Nothing," she said quickly, shaking her head. "We can head out whenever you're ready. I know you probably had plans."

Bleek leaned into her, and Mia held her breath as he whispered in her ear. "Plans change, and you are my plans for the evening. *You* come find me when you're ready to leave."

Mia exhaled loudly as he walked off and ran a hand down the front of her neck. Bleek had her hot! As he returned to the crowd, Mia couldn't deny what she felt for this man in such a short time. She saw him in a new, brighter light, not one she'd dreamed about. Yet, he still lived up to the image in her mind.

five

After another thirty minutes, Mia figured she'd head home for the evening. The event was wrapping up, and though Bleek told her he was on her time, Mia still wanted to be courteous. He'd given her enough of his time for the day. She held to-go food containers in her lap that Krypt urged her to take home.

Besides a granola bar while there and breakfast she'd eaten that morning, Mia was starving and couldn't wait to smash her plates. The sample of the dressing she and Moraye were given made her want to cry or kiss the chef it was so good. When her stomach growled loudly, her cheeks heated with embarrassment.

"That is so embarrassing," she groaned.

Bleek glanced her way and chuckled. "It's natural. My shit is touching my back, too."

"And you were lifting so many boxes. I know you're starving."

"I'm used to it. Long days at the shop be having me forget to eat. Today was really nice, though. Seeing folks smile and helping out. It reminded me of what really matters."

Mia nodded, studying his side profile as he spoke. His sincerity was disarming in the best way possible. She knew he wasn't trying to impress her, but he had.

"Yes, it's always a good time, and no one acts a fool," Mia said.

"That's a good thing. I 'preciate you for letting me be in your space today."

She melted in her seat.

"Of course. You were great with everyone," she said softly. "The kids, the families. It's like you've been doing this your whole life."

Bleek chuckled and smirked. "Might as well have been. My aunt Carletta, Jarod's mama, and my mama used to have us volunteering at the church and attending different events almost daily when we were growing up. We'd end up having more fun than we thought."

"Those are the best times," Mia said. "And it contributes to who you are."

So many people Mia interacted with on a daily basis lacked compassion, social skills, work ethic, and, more than anything, gratitude. It wasn't set in stone that volunteering cultivated who a person becomes, but it helped. She was grateful she and her brothers had the experience as well.

"Absolutely. Shout out to Ma Dukes and Auntie," he said, making her smirk

"They sound like great women."

Bleek's expression softened. "They are. Taught us rough-neck boys how to care for the people around us, even if it's something small. I guess it stuck with me."

She wanted to tell him it stuck with Jarod, too, because Grayce was well taken care of. Smiling, Mia rested her hand on his thigh.

"Well, I think they'd be proud. You were everything I didn't know I needed today."

Bleek glanced down at her hand and back up at the road. Feeling like she was playing with fire, Mia removed her hand.

"Crazily, I was thinking the same thing. You made the end of my work shift that I normally dread ten times better. I'ma have to tag along more often."

Mia chuckled. "It's not like you gave me a choice."

"You always have a choice, beautiful."

She swallowed hard at his words and cleared her throat. "True. You did kinda invite yourself, though."

"I did," he admitted, his grin widening. "But it worked out, didn't it?"

She shook her head, laughing. "Yes, it did."

"What you got planned for tomorrow?" Bleek asked.

He wondered if she could hear the thirstiness in his question. Mia's entire aura was a vibe, and he wanted to be in her presence. He didn't care that they'd just hung out for almost the entire day.

"Not much. Go by my mama's house and then my best friends. You?"

Family traditions hadn't been the same for years in her family. One brother lived out of state, the other had a grudge against the family, and Mia just wanted her daddy back. So, she'd typically stay home until late in the evening and then make her rounds. Every day wasn't a good day for her, but she tried her best to live in gratefulness. Some people didn't get to live until the next day, so she tried to make hers count.

"About the same. Ending it at my aunties crib with everybody," Bleek divulged as he pulled onto her street.

"That sounds nice. I'd normally have more plans, but you know… life of a single person."

Bleek chuckled. "Yeah, it's not too bad, but I'm glad you're single now. That means I can take you out."

Mia giggled. "Been waiting on your chance, huh?"

"Shiiit," Bleek dragged, making them laugh. "I mean, I wasn't pressed if that's what you're hinting at."

"I said no such thing," Mia teased, lifting her hands in surrender.

"It's coo' if you were. You're someone to be pressed over, beautiful. I promise you that."

His compliments were getting the best of Mia. Instead of going home, she was ready to tell him she'd ride with him anywhere he wanted to go. Hell, she'd ride his fine ass too.

"I believe you, but a date so soon?"

"What's the hold up?" Bleek asked. "You don't like going out?"

It wasn't that. Honestly, Mia didn't know what it was. She didn't have an answer to give him. When he realized she wasn't going to say anything, Bleek double-backed.

"My fault. Maybe I didn't come at you correctly," he said and cleared his throat. "I'd love to take you out, LaMia, if that's okay with you."

Unable to hide her blush, Mia smiled and said, "Yes, that's okay with me."

Bleek nodded. "Okay. Coo'."

Date night ideas were already forming in his head. He wasn't trying to force her into anything, but he could tell she needed a little convincing. Bleek found it odd, but he was a man of action. Words only held so much weight after a while.

Plus, it was a man's, a real man's, natural instinct to want to take a woman out, show her a good time, and be kind. A woman shouldn't have to beg or teach somebody's raggedy son that. Bleek's mother had raised a good man.

When he pulled up to her house, Mia frowned. She didn't recognize the black Lexus parked in her driveway. "Who is this?" she questioned, reaching inside her purse for her phone.

"I forgot to tell you. I had one of my homeboys drop off a loaner car," Bleek said coolly as if it were nothing.

And it wasn't. Stunned and damn near at a loss

for words, Mia turned to face him. She'd been having such a good time that she'd forgotten all about not having a vehicle. Bleek's consideration caught her off guard and brought tears to her eyes. After everything he'd done today, he still made a way to put another smile on her face and not let her go without.

She blinked back tears and said, "Bleek."

"LaMia." He grinned.

"This is too much. How did you... when did you even have time to do all that?"

Her sniffling and watery eyes were breaking his heart, but he knew she wasn't crying because she was sad. Bleek had made her day. Those were tears of pure joy.

"I have my ways. You needed a way to get around until your car is fixed, so here's a whip. I told you I had you."

Mia wiped away the stubborn tear that slid down her cheek. "You did, but—"

"No buts," he said, cutting her off. "I ain't trying to hear nothing, but you saying thank you, Bleek," he said, mocking her sultry voice he'd grown to love.

Mia laughed and playfully rolled her eyes. "I do not sound like that."

He smirked. "Close enough."

Wiping her eyes, Mia leaned his way. "Thank you, Bleek. I *really* do appreciate you."

Her appreciation was said with a kiss on his cheek. It was so damn close to the corner of his mouth that it took everything in him not to grab her by the chin and tongue her down. Something was telling him Mia wasn't ready for all that.

Licking his lips, Bleek leaned back in his seat, running a hand over his beard. "You're welcome."

"So, when should I come by to get my car and return this one?"

"More than likely Friday since Ryan ordered the part before clocking out, but whenever it's ready. Take my number down so you can get in contact with me."

Without overthinking it, Mia unlocked her phone. Going to her keypad, Bleek called out his digits, and she saved his number.

"Okay. I have you locked in, and I just texted you. I really can't thank you enough for today. I need to call your mama and let her know she didn't miss a beat raising you," Mia said, making them laugh.

"Aye. Credit to my Pops, too. He set the example."

Bleek immediately noticed her smile fade and her mood shift when his dad was mentioned. Not wanting to make the situation awkward, he broke the silence.

"And you were talking about me kidnapping you. Look who's holding who hostage," he jested.

Laughing, Mia unfastened her seatbelt. "Oh, hush. I'll get out of your funky lil' truck."

"Yeah, a'ight. Just don't touch that handle, and we're good."

When he climbed out to come around to her side, Mia blew out a breath. "Whew. This man," she said quietly, and the door opened. Bleek grabbed her food while she gathered a few bags she had retrieved from her car. She stuck her hand out to take her tray from him.

"You good to carry all this?" Bleek asked.

"It's just two bags and my purse," she chuckled. "Yes, I have it."

He looked at her arm and shook his head. "Nah. Come on. 'Cause how were you going to open the door and get the key to the car?"

Mia watched him walk off, and she stood there. "Well, I'll never know now." She laughed to herself and followed behind him.

Reaching on top of the front right wheel of the Lexus, Bleek grabbed the key fob and handed it to her. At the door, Mia unlocked it and stepped inside.

Placing her bags down, she turned to grab her food but wanted to hug him. He could see it all in her eyes when she thanked him again.

"Thank you," she said, going in for the hug.

Bleek held her around the waist and squeezed tight. "You're welcome," he said against her ear.

The feel of his warm breath and soft lips brushing against her earlobe made Mia shiver and break their embrace. Fucking him on the first night in her dream was one thing. Getting busted down in real life just to show him her gratitude was something different. Mia didn't have it in her, so her question at brunch last week was answered.

"Any plans for tonight?" She asked, taking a step back.

Bleek shook his head. "None tonight. Just kick back for a bit. Keep all my energy for tomorrow."

"Same. Well, I hope you enjoy the rest of your night. It was nice spending an unexpected day with you, Mr. Community Superstar."

He chuckled. "See there you go," he said and Mia grinned. "If you need anything before your car is ready, let me know."

"I can't think of anything right now, but I'll let you know if I do."

Bleek nodded once. "I'ma hold you to that. Have a good night, beautiful. Thank you for today."

A small smile tugged at her lips as he headed out the door. She waved when he honked twice and backed out of the driveway. Bleek waited until he was sure she'd locked the door before pulling off. Mia's day had taken an unexpected turn, but she wasn't complaining anymore. Spending time with Bleek felt right... it was right, and she was about to have an even better night. She hoped he came to her in her dreams again. The wet kind this time because she had fresh batteries and a vibrator waiting.

"Thank you, Bleek," she said and giggled.

six

Thanksgiving Day

"I know you aren't about to leave already?" Jasmine, Shay's mama, asked.

Mia smiled. "Yes. I'm a little sleepy. Plus, I have to run some errands in the morning."

After leaving her mama's house, which almost made her go right back home, Mia prep talked herself into a better mood and made it to Shay's house. She'd been there for two hours and was ready to call it a night. After working all week, volunteering, and helping Grayce prepare for tomorrow's big sale, Mia was dog-tired.

"Mama! Leave Mia alone. You know she's a homebody," Shay yelled from the kitchen.

Mia smirked. "Thank you, friend!"

"Oh, girl. Y'all ain't fooling me. You're probably about to go see some man about a horse."

"Oh my gosh!" Shay gagged, walking into the living room where they were. "Mama, for real. Please don't say that again."

Jasmine waved her off. "I'm grown, and so are y'all. Mia is my daughter; she can tell me if she was ditching us to go lay up."

Mia had to laugh. "Sadly, I'm not. But, when I do, you'll be the first to know."

Jasmine winked and sipped from the cup she'd been drinking out of since cooking this morning. "That's my girl. Love you, Mia. Drive safely."

"Love you, too," she called out. "Girl, you know your mama is a mess."

Shay rolled her eyes. "She gets on my nerves, honey. But for real. Where are you about to go?"

"Home," Mia said and laughed. "I wasn't lying. I'm tired and have to help Grayce tomorrow."

"That is right. Well, let me know when you make it in. I think I'ma go out. You know my cousins nem' throwing that All Black party downtown."

She'd heard about it and saw the flyers on social

media but had no intentions of going. Watching movies and eating her leftovers was her only plans.

"Yeah, I know. Have fun, and don't get too messed up. Call me if you need me," Mia said, and they hugged.

"I will. Love you, friend."

"I love you, too, girl."

Before she could pull away from the curb, Mia's phone rang. Seeing Bleek's name pop up with an incoming FaceTime call made her smile. They'd been texting and sending voice notes all day, so she had no idea what he could be calling for. But she answered just to see his face.

"Hello," she said and smiled.

Bleek was grinning in the screen, gorgeous dark skin all shiny, while his crisp line-up and waves greeted her. He licked his lips, and Mia noticed his low eyes.

"You so damn pretty," he blurted, making her blush. "Happy Thanksgiving."

"Thank you. Happy Thanksgiving to you, too."

"What you doing?" He wanted to know.

Mia's brows dipped. "I'm about to leave my best friend's house. You didn't get my text?"

Mia could've sworn she told him that's where she was at.

"Yeah, I got it. I asked what you were doing 'cause I can see you sitting in the car," Bleek explained.

"Oh," Mia quipped. "Well, I just got in the car when you called."

"Perfect timing, then. Pull up on me. I wanna see you."

She chuckled and panned the camera over her face and body. "You see me now."

Bleek's eyes lowered as he licked his lips. Mia looked real cute in a brown long sleeve body suit, and brown leather pants. The shirt had an exaggerated plunging V-neck that had her triple-D breasts looking too good for Bleek not to acknowledge.

"Yeah, I see you got them titties out. Why you ain't send me a picture?"

"Oh, my gosh," Mia laughed. "See how you act."

"Nah. That's you. You the one acting funny, LaLa. It's Thanksgiving, and you're not trying to give me what I want," Bleek teased, his tone charmful but not overbearing.

She laughed but could only focus on him calling her LaLa like he had in her dream. One thing was sure: he was persistent and consistent in real life, too. Mia lowkey loved it but was nervous.

"And what about what I want?" She asked.

"You can have anything you want. Just say the word, and it's yours."

His expression was serious, and his words were spoken clearly... warmly, hitting Mia right in the chest. He meant them. Bleek never just talked for the fuck of it.

"Tell me what you want, beautiful," Bleek urged.

"I want to see you, too. Maybe just for a little bit."

Mia was being vulnerable, but it felt okay.

"A'ight. Come see me then. Want me to shoot you the address or come and see you?"

"I'll pull up wherever you're at," she answered.

Bleek grinned, and Mia squeezed her legs shut. It was a shame to be this turned on through a Face-Time call with a man she technically just met, but she couldn't control it. Bleek possessed the kind of charm and commanding presence that made you yearn to be near him. Crazily, he felt that same way about Mia, so she had nothing to be worried about.

"It's just my people nem'. Nothing for you to be nervous about," Bleek told her.

She chuckled. "Mhm. We'll see. Text me the address, sir."

He pulled his bottom lip into his mouth and almost brazenly asked if he could eat her pussy in the back of his SUV when she pulled up, but kept it cool.

"What?" Mia asked, catching his gaze.

He shook his head. "Nothing, girl. You got me thinking some wild shit with your pretty ass."

"Is this the real you outside of work?"

"What you mean?" Bleek questioned.

"You're more... I don't know, yourself?"

He chuckled and ran a hand over his waves. "I'm the same real nigga three-sixty-five. You got the reserved me yesterday 'cause I was trying to keep it professional but fuck all that now. I want you. And I ain't talkin' 'bout just for tonight or the next day. So, when you get here don't be acting like we ain't have this conversation, 'cause I'm on your ass."

Mia gulped and blushed so damn hard that she made him smirk. "Um, yeah. I hear you. Send the address."

"I'm sending it right now," Bleek said, sharing his location.

"Got it. You gon' hang up?"

He laughed. "Look at you. Ready to speed your ass over here. I ain't going anywhere, baby. Take your time."

Playfully, she rolled her eyes. "I mean, I can go home."

"Nah." He straightened up. "Don't do that. 'Cause then I'ma have to explain to my mama why I left without saying bye like she raised a heathen."

"Not you ready to leave and come to my house."

"Be parked outside that bitch like the feds."

Laughter filled her car, and Mia shook her head. Suddenly, she wasn't tired at all and ready to do the dash to see her boo. It's so funny how quickly circumstances and titles change.

* * *

"Mama, this is LaMia. LaMia, this is my mama, Gwen."

When Bleek walked outside to open her car door, hugged her like he'd been away at sea for months, and kissed her, Mia didn't think the first person she'd be introduced to was his mother. She was trying to fuck this woman's son down to the ground and get stuffed, not exchange names.

"Hi," Mia smiled, trying to ignore Bleek's hand on her waist. "It's nice to meet you."

Gwen leaned in, giving her a warm hug, and Mia reciprocated. "Nice to meet you, too, sweetie. You're the one he went and served the community with yesterday?"

"Yes," Mia said and glanced up at him. "I heard it's a favorite thing of his to do."

It was Gwen's turn to look at her son. "Since a youngin', but I hadn't heard about him going in a while. You must be something special, I see."

Mia chuckled. "I'm guessing so."

"Well, no need to guess with this one. He's very upfront and will let you know what it is and what it isn't," Gwen said.

Bleek smirked. "And who did I get that from?"

"That damn daddy of yours. Let me go find my husband. Mia, don't be shy. It's plenty of food and drinks," she said before walking toward the basement.

"I won't. Thank you," Mia said.

Bleek gripped her waist and turned her to face him. "You good?"

She smiled. "Yes. Are you? You're so touchy today."

"I'm doing too much?"

She giggled and shook her head. "No. It's fine. Just behave."

Quickly, Mia kissed his lips. She wasn't quick enough because Bleek wrapped her in a hug and nastily tongued her down right in the foyer of his aunties home. He sucked on her tongue and squeezed her ass. Mia moaned into his mouth just as one of his uncles walked by.

"A'ight, nephew! I see you."

Bleek took his time pulling away, using his thumb to wipe the extra shine from her bottom lip. "I been wanting to feel and taste those pretty lips since I met you."

"A year ago?" Mia asked in a whisper.

"A year ago," he confirmed.

Mia smirked. "Call me crazy, but you're giving me every reason to fall for you. What's up your sleeve, sir?"

She took a slight step back and stared at him. Bleek looked beyond good and smelled even better. He had on black jeans, a crisp black t-shirt, a caramel-colored jacket, and a fresh pair of stylish shoes Mia didn't know the name of.

"There's nothing up my sleeve. You heard my mama. I'm upfront with any and everything. If you fall, you fall, baby. It won't be alone."

"Good to know. Now, can we move from here and stop giving people a show."

"Shit, you lucky I ain't slide my hand in them tight ass pants and see how wet I got you," he said, smacking her ass.

Mia blushed and swatted his hand. "Behave."

Bleek chuckled. "Yeah, a'ight."

The first stop was the kitchen, where Mia was introduced to everyone and handed his aunt Moniece the bottle of wine she'd brought. She'd eaten and taken a to-go plate from Shay's, but the smell of turkey and sweet potato pie tempted her to make another plate. And she did just that once she saw the baked macaroni and cheese and greens. Bleek tried to sit beside her while she ate so she wouldn't feel out of place, but the ladies shooed him away.

It'd been a while since Bleek brought someone to meet his family, so all the women were gushing over her, trying to see what she'd done to him. She hadn't done a thing but be herself, and Bleek liked that about her the most. She didn't put up a front to impress him, nor would she ever need to. It hadn't even been a full forty-eight hours, and he was ready to lock Mia's ass down.

After she finished eating, they headed to the basement, where more family was, and Mia couldn't help but feel emotional. They were so close-knit and embraced her as if she were family. The little cousins asked her to do TikTok dances, while the women her age included her in conversation and didn't act like she wasn't there. Bleek watched Mia mingle with his people, seamlessly fitting in. It was as if she'd been part of the fold for years.

He heard the tremble in her voice when she answered his question about her plans for the day. Bleek didn't want her to ever feel like she had to be alone on the holidays or at all, so that was one of the reasons he invited her over. He knew his family would make her feel loved and welcomed.

Mia was trying to take it all in when one of the little cousins who'd been glued to her hip said, "What are you thankful for, Miss Mia?"

So caught up in her own world, Mia hadn't thought that far yet. Every year, it was a tradition in the King family to go around the room and say what they were thankful for. No one got a pass, guest or not. There was always something to be grateful for, even if you didn't think so. Living to see another day was a blessing on its own.

Groans and laughs echoed through the room when each family began sharing what they were thankful for. One of the older aunts expressed her gratitude for her growing business, which she started at age forty-six. His cousin Boubie cracked a joke about being grateful for a winning football season even though they were playing like shit, and Bleek's mom tearfully talked about the joy of having everyone together. She was the more emotional one out of her siblings.

Bleek was across the room from Mia, who looked slightly nervous but tried to play it cool when it was her turn. She didn't mind sharing, but she had never done so in front of strangers who didn't feel like strangers. All eyes fell on her.

"I'm thankful for... knowing my worth and spending the evening with the sweetest people who reminded me what it feels like to belong and just be. So, thank y'all, for real. It means a lot to me," she said, her voice soft but confident.

Across the room, Bleek gave her a small, knowing smile before blowing her a kiss.

"Aye, man," one of his cousins said. "Mia got this man blowing kisses. Get 'em out of here."

The room broke out in laughter, but Bleek didn't feel the least bit embarrassed about being called out.

"I'd be disrespectful if I did what I *really* wanted to do in front of y'all," he said, and Gwen shook her head.

"Baby, get your son," she laughed, talking to her husband, Derrick.

He smirked at Bleek. "At least he's telling the truth. Who's next?"

The family went around the room, and Mia held her breath when it was Bleek's turn. She quickly learned that he spoke from the heart, and she was a little nervous about what he'd say.

He cleared his throat. "Good evening, family," he said. "Y'all looking real nice tonight."

"Boy! Come on, nie," Moniece yelled. "I'm ready to get back to my card game. You know it's fifty-leven of us, hell."

"See, auntie. I was gonna say I'm grateful for you, but never mind."

Everyone cracked up, and Moniece flipped him off. Mia was having a time and wondered when Grayce and Jarod were coming. The last she checked, they were having dinner with Grayce's family. She made a mental reminder to check her phone and then focused on Bleek.

"Nah, all jokes aside. I joke and get my laughs off, but I'm very thankful for everyone in this room. So much good has happened this year for our family, and y'all have held me down in ways I can't even explain. I'm thankful for the shop for keeping me busy and grounded. And..."

His gaze shifted to Mia, and it stayed.

"I'm thankful for unexpected blessings. For

people who remind me that good things can happen when you least expect them to."

The room quieted for a beat, and one of his cousins nudged Mia. "That's your cue, girl."

Her cheeks flushed, and she smiled. Bleek's words couldn't have been more valid. The people near them laughed, and Bleek shook his head.

"Y'all are too much."

They glanced at one another from across the room, and something unspoken was shared between them. Mia wasn't sure if it was an acknowledgment, a promise, or maybe even a beginning, but she felt it, and Bleek did, too.

As the evening winded down, the family shared stories, ate more desserts, took a few shots while playing games, and just enjoyed one another. For the first time in a long time, Mia felt like she was exactly where she was supposed to be.

Feeling her phone vibrate at the last minute, she pulled it out of her purse where it'd been for most of the night. Her heart sank when she saw a missed call and a voicemail. Standing up, she headed for the steps and Bleek called after her.

"LaLa!"

She turned on her heels. "I'm fine. Just gotta take this call," she said and rushed up the steps.

Bleek's forehead creased with worry, but he didn't get up. He inserted himself into her life, so of course, she had other things going on. So, he wasn't trying to do too much. Still, he wondered what or who had her rushing out of there.

Once Mia got upstairs, she asked if there was some place quiet she could talk on the phone. One of the cousins had her follow them to one of the spare bedrooms and told her they hoped everything was okay. Mia hoped so, too. Going to her voicemail, she held her breath as she placed play.

"Baby girl. It's your daddy," Benny chuckled. "Happy Thanksgiving, daughter. I know you're probably wondering why I haven't called you in some weeks and it's because I was in the hole. I'm not trying to get into all that, though. I just wanted to hear your voice and see what all you ate today. I know you went over Shay's. Her mama still makes that nasty green bean casserole?"

Mia cackled because, yes... she did. She made it every year, even though no one touched it but she and one other person. She'd taken him a plate of it one year, and Benny told her if she loved him, to never bring him shit else from Shay's mama. Thankfully, Shay could throw down in the kitchen and learned from her other side of the family.

"Man, that shit was horrible. Tell Shay I said what's up. I don't have much longer, but you know I was going to call you when I could. I hope you're sticking to your guns and not fooling with that ungrateful ass nigga you were with. But I know you aren't. Once you're done with something, you're done. I love that about you, baby girl."

Mia sniffled and smiled. Benny knew her so well.

"You get that trait from your mama. She still acting like she doesn't love me, but it's all good. When I get out, I'ma see what she talking about."

Laughing, Mia shook her head. Her mama wasn't worried about him at all. They'd broken up years ago and it would remain that way.

"There's a lot to be thankful for Mia. Even though I'm in here, I haven't lost my faith. I don't want you to lose yours either. Don't take people or any situation in life for granted. Cherish every moment, a'ight? You're a gift, baby girl. The rarest kind, and you deserve someone who knows that. Don't let these men out here get a pass because you feel lonely. That shit doesn't last forever. Keep your head up, Snooks. Be safe tonight, and I'll call you tomorrow. I love you."

The voicemail ended, and Mia couldn't control her tears. Hearing him call her by her childhood nickname had her bawling. She'd been waiting for over a month to get a call from him, so missing it made her sick to her stomach. Benny had been in prison for four years for murder, but it felt like he'd just gone in yesterday.

He and Mia were out shopping one afternoon when a random man at the mall physically assaulted her. Benny was sitting outside one of the stores waiting for her, and when she rushed out in a panic, telling him what had happened, the rest was history. Mia suggested they go to the security and the police hub inside the mall, but Benny wasn't trying to hear that.

They followed him out of the mall, and Benny immediately began to beat his ass. When he saw the man draw a gun, he pulled his too and was quicker, ending his life. In court, they claimed it wasn't self-defense, and Mia taking the stand to report that he assaulted her wasn't justified to kill a man in cold blood. Benny didn't see it that way, and neither did Mia. They knew the man would've walked free if the roles were reversed.

The entire situation still broke Mia's heart to this day. She was a daddy's girl. Being unable to physically have him in her life sometimes made her bitter. She blamed herself a lot, and Benny hated that she did. He laid a man down for disrespecting his daughter and lost his freedom, and he would do it all over again if he had to. It was just how he got down.

Mia was so deep in her feelings she didn't even hear Bleek knocking on the door. She only noticed he had come looking for her when he sat on the bed beside her.

"Awww man. Come here," he cooed, pulling her into his arms.

Bleek didn't say anything, he just let her loosely hug him and cry. He rubbed her back and waited until she was settled down to ask what he'd been wanting to know since he entered the room.

"Whose ass do I need to beat for making you cry like this?"

Mia chuckled and lifted her head from his chest. "I don't think you can whoop my daddy, so..."

"He's a man just like me. What happened?" Bleek asked.

Sighing, Mia debated if she wanted to share something so intimate with him. It wasn't anything new, and you could look his case up, but still. It was a touchy subject to bring to the table early on, but she also figured if he couldn't handle her at her worse, then he damn sure couldn't at her best.

So, she gave him the short version. The way Bleek clenched his fists and the way his jaw flexed when she said someone assaulted her made an invisible blanket of protection wrap around her. Bleek would protect her with his life, and he didn't have to say anything for her to know it.

"Yeah, so... that's why I'm in here with raccoon eyes," Mia jested, trying to lighten the mood.

Bleek kept the same energy. "At least you're a pretty raccoon. Them mothafuckas is ugly."

She chuckled and shook her head. "I'll take what I can get."

"How you feeling now? A good cry is cleansing for the soul."

"I feel okay, but I want to go home. I was already tired before getting here, and crying exhausted me. Plus, my mood is shitty. I don't want to bring that around everyone," Mia said.

Bleek nodded. "A'ight. I feel that. Just so you know, you're Pops is a real nigga. Any real man would've done what he had in his shoes. You still get to talk to him and visit instead of crying over his grave, so that's a bright side to it."

He didn't want to say anything wrong but had to tell her what it was. Mia didn't take his words wrong at all.

"Yes, I know. He'd like that you're trying to make me think about the positive side of this," she chuckled.

"See. Even he knows it."

Mia sighed and then unintentionally yawned. "Ooh. Excuse me."

"You're good. Did you enjoy my people tonight?"

She smiled and nodded. "I did so much. Your family is a mess but so loving. One of them asked me if they could spend the night with me since you're their favorite cousin and I'm your girlfriend."

Bleek chuckled. "Shit, sleepover at Mia's crib, then."

She hadn't had a sleepover in so long; the idea didn't sound bad at all. Not with his little cousins, though. Just Bleek... and on a night where she was in a better mood. It was hard to shake.

"I love how we all had to say what we were thankful for," she said.

"Yeah. We do it every year and someone records it. It reminds us throughout the year to think back on all the good and even the bad 'cause it got us to another day."

Mia nodded, loving that mindset. "That's so true."

"And I meant what I said earlier, too." She faced

him and Bleek swiped the curls that fell into her face. "You've got this quiet strength, La. I peeped it when you were at the shop. I know I may be coming on a little strong—"

"You're not," she said, cutting him off.

He nodded. "A'ight. But I just want you to know that I want to be someone who adds to that strength. Not someone who takes away from it and causes more stress."

His words hit her deeper than she expected them to. Mia's core trembled at the vulnerability on the brightest display right now. It was...bonding them in a way she knew would last.

"You just don't know how much stress you've relieved me of since yesterday. Seriously, why does it feel like two days have felt like I've known you my entire life?"

Bleek shrugged. "Serendipity? We were meant to cross paths again, not just briefly."

Mia had to agree. "I'm with you when you're right."

"What time do you have to be up in the morning?" Bleek asked.

She yawned again, covering her mouth. "Um, I think Grayce... wait." She stopped mid-sentence to check her phone. Grayce had texted her asking where she was five minutes ago. Mia hurriedly texted her back and told her she was about to leave.

"That's her?" Bleek questioned.

"Mhm. They just got here. But, I think nine-ish. I'ma find out when we go out here."

Bleek told her okay and stood up. Mia followed suit and exhaled.

"Did I tell you how fine you looked today?" she asked.

He smirked. "Nah. You were too busy jeffing with my mama."

"I was not jeffing," she laughed, smacking his arm. "Quiet as kept, she loves me already."

"Yeah, I bet. You going straight to sleep when you get home?"

Mia eyed him suspiciously. "After I shower and decompress, more than likely. Why?"

"If you can't sleep, call me."

Her bottom lip jutted out. "Bleek, please, okay. I like you. You don't have to lay it on any thicker."

Bleek chuckled. Pulling her into his arms, he sucked on her bottom lip and hugged her. "I'ma lay it on as thick as you can take it. How 'bout that?"

"You're going to do what you want to see me smile, so whatever," she chuckled.

"I'm glad you know. Come on."

Opening the door, he let her walk out first. When they entered the living room, Grayce was sitting on the sofa and hopped up. She squinted at Bleek and Mia laughed.

"He didn't do anything," she said and they hugged.

"Oh, okay, because I was about to say. Me and his family will jump him," Grayce said.

Bleek waved her off. "I can't believe it's like that, G."

"Behind this one," she said, pointing at Mia. "It's always like that. With whoever. Now, where are you going?" She asked, facing her friend.

Bleek couldn't do anything but respect it. While they chatted, he and Jarod dapped hands and caught one another up on everything they'd missed. Specifically, the football game that was on. It was crazy how, two years ago, neither had women with them at their aunt's house. Now, they were dating— Jarod was in a relationship— and Bleek hoped he and Mia's relationship progressed to that level.

After saying bye to everyone and assuring Grayce that she'd see her in the morning, Bleek walked Mia to her car. She did feel much better now, but she was still tired.

"Text me when you get home," Bleek said,

standing outside her door. She had the window rolled down while her car warmed up.

"I will. Thank you for inviting me today. Maybe we can make this a tradition," she suggested.

Bleek loved the sound of that. "You ain't trying to keep me around that long," he joked.

"Says who? You just saw me ugly cry. Boy, you're stuck with me."

That pulled a laugh from them both.

"Whatever you say, beautiful. Drive safely."

"Wow. I get tongued down when I get here and can't get a kiss goodbye?"

Pulling her door open, Bleek wrapped her in a bear hug that made Mia laugh. Then, he gave her the sweetest, most soul-stirring, reconsider her entire life, type of kiss she'd never gotten from a man. Mia was breathless when he pulled away. Her chest heaved while she looked at him as if he'd just delivered the stars and the moon to her doorstep.

"Bleek," she whispered.

He smirked. "LaMia," he said. "I know, baby. I feel that shit, too."

She shook her head. "I'm...I'm going to text you when I get home."

"A'ight. I'ma text back."

Mia smiled as he shut her door and tapped the

hood. He stepped out of the street, and she pulled off. A million and one thoughts ran through her mind on her way home, and she couldn't sort any of them out. The main one being how the man literally from her dreams was becoming hers in real life.

"I'm *so* thankful," she said, smiling.

seven

Mia had been home for less than two hours when Bleek received a text asking if he wanted to come over. She hit him up when she entered her house, but Mia knew she didn't want to end her night without him beside her. She'd stuck to her morals and didn't fuck him last night, but today was a new day.

"What kind of wine were you sipping before I got here?" Bleek asked, trailing kisses down her neck.

Her skin smelled of cashmere and cocoa butter. A scent that had Bleek ready to eat her off the fucking bone like an oxtail.

"Just a glass of *Divine*," she moaned.

Great taste, Bleek thought. He knew the brand's

owner, Shyriq Hendrix, and made a mental reminder to keep her bottles stocked.

The wine made her feel lovely, as did the bath that she took. All that food, the crying, and the day had all been washed away. Now, all she needed was for Bleek to act like he knew what he came here for. He was moving much too slowly for her liking.

"Bleek," she whined as he massaged her breasts.

"Yes, LaMia? Can I take my time with you, or you trying to get fucked straight to sleep and made love to in the wee hours of the morning?"

She shuddered at his question and the way he tweaked and pinched her nipples. Mia couldn't answer him and forgot what she was whining for when his hand slid between her legs. She was most definitely going to let him take his time. The silk robe she had on slipped from her naked frame, pooling at her feet.

"Both," she said, finally recollecting his words.

Stepping around her, Bleek's hands caressed her body. He had to take a minute to cherish it and her. He kissed down her chest and soft belly where a piercing was, all while sensually massaging her ass cheeks. Mia's eyes rolled when he placed the juiciest kiss against her lower lips.

Bleek was grateful she kept the lights on and

wasn't trying to hide from him. He should've known that a woman with such a beautiful soul had the pussy to match. Like an examiner, he spread her puffy lips, exposing her clit that was practically screaming for him to suck in like his favorite candy. But he waited... only giving it a firm lick that curled Mia's pink toes.

Looking up, Bleek caught her watching his every move. He slid a finger inside of her and watched her reaction. Mia's mouth fell open as he stroked her a few times, and it blew his mind how disgustingly wet she was.

Her thighs were soaked, and he hadn't done much yet. Needing to taste her, Bleek removed his finger and sucked it clean. Then, he slipped his tongue inside Mia's mouth for her to taste. When she moaned, he smirked and broke their lip lock.

"Mhm. Pussy tastes like you should've been the only thing getting eaten today."

Bleek knew in his gut that he was off the market after tonight. The way he already felt himself craving Mia was intense, but after tasting her... no other woman mattered. Mia let him lead her to her bed, and he patted her on the ass. She knew what that meant but loved how he still instructed her.

"Bend over and don't move."

She sank her knees into the memory foam mattress, spread them apart, and arched her back. The most content sigh came from her as she rested her head with nothing but anxiousness flowing through her veins. This view from behind made Bleek shake his head and remove the *SILK* condom from his sweatpants before stripping from them and his briefs.

When Mia left his aunt's house, so did he mentally before departing physically thirty minutes later. Once he was home, he stroked one out in the shower with Mia on his mind, so she was about to get straight second-wind dick.

Bleek trailed his thumbs down her spine, applying pressure with a subtle massage. His lips followed suit. His kisses were so tender and reassuring she squeezed her eyes tight and pressed back into him. When he got to her round ass, Bleek spread her cheeks and dragged his tongue down her crack. Mia's stomach caved as he licked, slurped, and probed her asshole. Then, he went lower and did the same to her clit. His tongue flickered her bud before suctioning it.

"Bleek... oh my gosh. Please!" She was begging, and he wanted to know why.

"Please, what, hmm?"

He took a break from indulging to ask but never got an answer. Mia couldn't speak. All she knew was that she wanted him to keep doing exactly what he was doing. His tongue swirled, lapping at her juices that wouldn't stop flowing. Her soft moans only encouraged him to keep going as if they were a chant. She was vocal with it, and Bleek loved that shit.

"Mmmmhhmmm." He hummed with the utmost satisfaction as if savoring the best meal... and she was the fucking best. Nothing but Michelin Stars across the board.

His loud slurps echoed throughout the room, and Bleek didn't come from between her legs until she was a trembling, creamy mess. Mia struggled to catch her breath, muffling gasps while squeezing the life out of a pillow. Bleek stood back admiring her, running a hand over her ass before gently caressing her pussy and patting it.

"Pussy that good gon' get me in trouble, beautiful," Bleek rasped.

Mia's hearing slowly returned in waves. It fizzled out as she climaxed, making her almost certain that he'd taken her to another planet. And he wasn't done touring yet. Lying her on her back, Bleek hovered over her with a dick so hard he couldn't think straight. She looked so flustered and pretty, with hair all over her head and fluttering eyelids.

"Mmm, hi," she greeted in a moaning tone, running her hands down her body.

Bleek smirked. "What's up, beautiful."

"Come here. You're too far away."

Sliding his shirt off, Bleek slid the condom on and climbed on the bed. Lifting her with ease, he moved them up the bed and settled between her legs. Mia ran a hand over his face, taking in his handsome features. He was so fine it was unfair.

She pulled him closer by the back of his neck and spread her legs wider. Mia licked the shell of his ear and gripped his dick, placing it at her entrance. Slowly, she pushed him inside of her, and her eyes immediately watered.

"Sss. Fuck," she cried and gasped as he sank further.

Bleek expanded her walls, delivering measured strokes so she could get comfortable with his size. He was blessed, but so was she, as Mia took him fully. Her pussy was showing her just how accommodating she could be as it stretched for him. Bleek released the deepest groan, frustrated and so gotdamn appreciative of how amazing she felt.

"Fuck," he hissed lowly, eyes closing.

Pressing her thighs into the mattress, Bleek slid in and out of her wet pussy with pleasure etching his handsome face. The condom did nothing to shield her wetness that engulfed him. It was as if he had nothing on, and that was dangerous. Even more dangerous than the sultry look she was giving him as he placed her ankles on his shoulders and stroked her with precision. This new angle made Mia suck in a deep breath.

"Don't... don't look at me like that," Bleek urged.

Mia pulled him deeper into her and bit her lip. "Like what," she cooed.

Bleek shook his head, trying not to bust. Her voice, her snugness, the way she was fucking him back and moaning his name had him almost there.

"You feel so good," Mia moaned as they kissed.

Missionary with straight dick in her guts while tongue kissing was the quickest way to fall in love, and Mia knew it. She felt it with each plunge. Their skin slapped as Bleek pounded into her, giving her exactly what she needed. He was trying to fuck the stress, worry, and sadness up out of her. It was more to life than that, and maybe some A1 dick from a real one was the remedy Mia needed.

"I knew this pussy was good, beautiful. You gon' come for me?"

Mia nodded in the crook of his neck. Licking it, she sucked on it, trying to leave her mark. It wouldn't show on his dark skin, but Bleek would always know she'd been there. She'd engraved her name all over his dick, his mind, and with ease on his heart where he wanted her to stay.

"Baby," Mia whimpered.

Bleek licked his lips and sucked on her nipples while going deeper. He could feel his nut right there as her legs shook. He held onto her as she trembled, and her eyes rolled. When his back stiffened, and dick grew harder, a guttural groan escaped him.

"Shit," Bleek huffed, squeezing her waist.

Lowering her legs, he buried his head in her neck. His heavy panting sounded like a lullaby to Mia, and her body relaxed under his. His body atop hers was a customized heating blanket. She rubbed the back of his neck and down his back, feeling him smile against her skin.

"What're you smiling for?" she asked quietly.

"You keep squeezing my dick."

"She's saying thank you."

Bleek laughed, and she smirked before gasping

as he pumped into her, still hard. Mia didn't even know how that was possible, but it was.

"That was me telling her thank you, too. Never been more grateful in my life."

The morning after she had a wild night, Mia normally regretted it. They didn't come often anymore, as she was intentional with how she moved. Last night, though... she didn't consider that reckless at all. It was just right. Damn near perfection if there was such a thing.

As promised, Bleek delivered slow strokes to her center from the side in the wee hours of the morning. The shit felt so good that Mia couldn't even open her eyes. Somehow, they ended up in the shower afterward before falling into a deep sleep. Bleek held her all night right against his chest, pulling her closer to him whenever she moved. Mia didn't even think he knew what he was doing until he whispered, "Come here. I got you."

She smiled, recalling those words, and stretched out in her bed. Then, she frowned. Not feeling Bleek next to her, Mia shot up in the bed and looked around her room. She knew good and gotdamn well he hadn't left without saying anything.

"Where is he at?" she mumbled.

Grabbing her phone, Mia unlocked it and was about to call him when an incoming call derailed her plans.

Huffing with frustration, she answered. "Hello."

"Good morning. This is Rus with King's Auto. May I speak with LaMia."

"Good morning. This is she."

The sounds of paper shuffling came through the receiver before Rus said, "Good, good. Your vehicle is ready to pick up."

Mia frowned. "Already?"

"Yes, ma'am," the older gentleman said. His voice reminded Mia of her grandfathers.

"Oh. Okay," Mia said, surprised. "Can you tell me how much everything is, please?"

"Not a penny out of your pocket, sweetheart. Bellamy covered the tab."

She drew her head back. "I'm sorry, who?"

Rus chuckled. "You'll have to excuse me. I forget that he goes by Bleek. Hell is a Bleek," he quipped, making Mia chuckle. "But Bellamy is the owner. Your maintenance is on the house."

Mia didn't know what to say. "Wow. Okay. Thank you. I'll be by to get it soon."

"Un, huh, Sure thing. Have a good day now," Rus said and hung up.

Stupefied, Mia pressed her back against the headboard, pulling the covers around her naked frame. Bleek meant what he said when he told her he had her. She knew little about cars, but an alternator plus labor didn't seem like a cheap bill. When she picked her phone up to see where he was, and hopefully not get interrupted this time, she heard noise from the front of her house. A minute later, Bleek stepped through her bedroom door.

He smiled, carrying a plastic bag in one hand and an assortment of pink carnations wrapped in the prettiest paper and pink bow. Mia tucked her lips, wondering if he knew what they symbolized. He had to... that was just in his nature to know. *Or find out,* Mia thought. He was much to thoughtful to have just gotten them on a whim.

"Good morning, beautiful. Damn, you look good," Bleek praised, ready to pounce on her.

He'd fucked the bonnet off her head at three this morning, and her hair was a flirty mess that he loved.

"Bellamy," Mia said, blinking slowly.

Bleek chuckled and cracked a smile. He already knew she must've talked to Rus. The old man was the only one who didn't call him Bleek. It was okay, though. He was an OG who'd been working at the King's shops for decades.

She had so much more to say, but the way he stood there unbagging their food made Mia lose her train of thought. He looked so fine with a white tank top and black sweats on, with a black du-rag tied around his head. She could get used to waking up to him.

"Don't say my name like that, baby. I brought us some breakfast while I was out, but you got me ready to suck on that pussy just so I can hear you moan it."

And she'd let him do just that, but first, she had to get some things off her chest.

"I just spoke with Rus," she said.

"Yeah? What was he talking about?"

Mia scratched her head, watching him walk over to her. He placed the flowers on her lap and then kissed her lips. Morning breath and all, Bleek didn't care.

"Why are you talking as if he called about noth-ing?" she asked.

Bleek shrugged. "Because he did. It is nothing.

I'm a giver, baby. That's just something you gon' have to accept fucking with me."

Seeing the tears in her eyes, Bleek lifted her and the flowers before sitting down and placing her on his lap. As tall as she was, Mia felt so small in his arms. She felt safe. He created that space for her without thought and it had her ready to break down.

"We ain't crying today," he said, kissing her glossy eyelids.

She chuckled. "I'm just so appreciative, and I don't want to seem ungrateful by asking you why, but I can't help it. I've been a needy mess, and we just met."

"Need me, a'ight? Be okay with that. It ain't hurting shit. I want you to call on me for any and everything, knowing I got you. You were supposed to be mine long before now, so I'm making up for lost time. I'm not sure what happened in your last relationship, but don't let his fuck ups have you out here, believing you don't deserve the best. You do, and I'ma give it to you. Can you let me do that?"

Mia nodded. It was uncanny how much he sounded like her daddy, and Bleek hadn't heard the voicemail he left.

Bleek shook his head and said, "No, answer me. Let me hear you say it."

"I can let you do that," she answered, smiling.

"Do what?"

She blushed and tossed her head back. "You're going to make me say everything?"

"I'm 'bout to have you screaming my name in here real soon, so gon' head."

Sighing, Mia said, "I deserve this. I deserve you, and I won't let what happened in my last relationship hinder our growth. And even though I have a hard time accepting things, I'm going to try my best not to question why you give me things. It's just who you are. Your heart is big... and that dick is bigger," she said lowly and smirked.

Bleek shook his head and grinned. "Look at you. It got you talking crazy."

"Should've never given it to me," she said and shrugged. "I mean it, though. No more questioning you."

"Good. Now gimmie a kiss and come eat. Unless you trying to sit on my face."

He wiggled his eyebrows, and Mia laughed, hiding her face in his neck. This was his second time mentioning it, and she didn't want to deprive him any longer. Standing up, she groaned when her phone fell on the ground and hit her toe. When she leaned over to pick it up and heard someone hollering her name, she realized a call was connected. Her heart dropped, and she frowned, seeing an unsaved number, but Mia knew it could only be one person.

"What the hell?" She mumbled.

"What's wrong?" Bleek asked, seeing the spooked look on her face.

She held up her phone to show him the screen and mouthed, *this is my ex.*

Bleek bobbed his head forward, urging her to put him on speaker. She knew this could end badly, but Mia put him on speaker anyway.

"Hello?"

"Damn, Mia. It's like that? It's coo'. It really ain't no future for us after hearing that shit. You don't have to worry about me calling your phone ever again. On my mama. You foul."

Before she could respond, Kaleb hung up. Blinking, Mia looked up at Bleek and busted out laughing.

"What the hell was that?" She wheezed with tears in her eyes.

Bleek chuckled. "Hell if I know. You must've accidentally answered his call. You cold, baby."

"Oh well. That's his fault. I told him to stop

calling me months ago. You see, it was an unknown number," Mia explained.

"He got the message now."

She sighed and tossed her phone on the bed. "I hope so. Now... are you going to give me what I want?"

Mia straddled his lap, wrapping her arms around his neck.

"That's how I want you to talk from now on," he said, squeezing her booty. "I'ma give you everything you want plus more."

Mia believed him. She hadn't understood it before now, but giving really was a gift some people didn't deserve.

The End!

afterword

I hope you enjoyed Mia & Bellamy's cute story. I had
so much fun writing it.
There were a few couples mentioned in this book. If
you want to read about them, their books are listed
below.

Aspen & Ty - F**king Under The Mistletoe
Grayce & Jarod - Spin 'Bout You
Moraye & Adrien - Trappin' Through The Snow

FRO is a fictional Black-owned bookstore turned
brand by me. You can read about it in Yours To Have.